MOMENTS OF TRUTH

A Tour of the Other Side

NANCY J BALMERT

Nancy J Balmert

Copyright 2012, 2013, 2015, 2020, 2025

Nancy J Balmert

Fifth edition

ISBN: 978-0615683553

Cover design: Richard Windberg

To my AMAZING and FABULOUS husband Paul,
my one and only, the love of my life.

CONTENTS

ACKNOWLEDGMENTS

I want to thank Jesus for imparting all this incredible information to me from the Other Side and for allowing me to share it with those who are interested. I also want to thank God and my many Guardian Angels who have watched over me and helped me in this endeavor.

Then there are many, many on this side who have en-couraged me and supported me. Finally, a special thanks to my husband, who is a Saint for helping me in so many ways, including editing this book.

CHAPTER ONE

The Angels Came

Looking back on my near-death experience, I don't think I fit the type. You know: the wild eyed, out there type you see interviewed on TV, who goes around telling everyone, "I'm important because I had a near death experience. You better listen to what I have to tell you."

My life has been good, but 11/11 aside, it's hardly been the kind of life that makes for an exciting book. I didn't plan to be an author. Writing is definitely not my forte. I'd rather talk your ear off than sit and write. But I made a promise to Jesus that I'd share what I've learned, and writing a book happens to be one way to do that.

At the time of my near-death experience, I was a stay at home Mom, with two teenage boys, and a husband with a good career. This was the last thing in the world I ever imagined happening.

I can't say "Why did this happen to me?" I know exactly why it happened to me: I asked for it!

Well, not exactly. I didn't want to die or come anywhere close. I just wanted to understand the truth about life. Ultimately, that's what got me to where I'm now, writing a book about what happened– and what came about because of it. Now, I'm writing about what I've learned

When I meet someone new, and they often ask, "What do you do?" When I tell them I'm working on a book about my near- death experience, you'd be amazed at how often my newfound friend confides in me all about their own experience with the Other Side. My experience is that the unusual is a lot more usual than most of us seem to realize. It's not unusual to see a ghost, a loved one from the Other Side, have an out of body experience, or even a near death experience.

Often the person telling me their private story – a perfect stranger - hasn't told anyone in their family about the experience because they fear they wouldn't be believed. Many people simply feel safer by not sharing their own unusual experience. They don't choose to take the risk of someone making fun of them or not believing them. A few years ago, I went to a family reunion, and was in the middle of telling one of my cousins about my near-death experience, when one of her brothers came up to say hello. My cousin told him I had had a near-death experience; the first thing he did was to roll his eyes, implying I'm an idiot. That ended the conversation.

But often, the minute someone finds out that I've had a near death experience, they instantly feel comfortable sharing with me what happened to them. They feel safe and trust that I won't roll my eyes at them, and they'll know that I'll believe their story. I always do.

It happens all the time.

So, here's my story.

• • • • • • • •

November 11, 1996. I rolled out of bed, put on my exercise clothes, and headed out the door for my walk on a beautiful brisk Fall morning in Houston. When I returned, my husband left for work, and I attacked the Monday morning housecleaning with a vengeance. I was hosting the Garden Club at our house that week, and I wanted everything to be perfect.

So far, nothing unusual.

I'd been working in the yard all week preparing the flowerbeds and planting pansies for the winter. I decided to start putting the mulch out by the side of the house. I got the wheelbarrow and filled it with fresh bark mulch. It was a gorgeous day: sun shining, more like a Seattle summer day, although it was a Houston November day. There was the slightest breeze that rustled in the trees and the birds were singing. It was so beautiful out and I was enjoying the incredible day.

I pulled the wheelbarrow up and knelt onto the ground. I reached into the wheelbarrow to get a handful of mulch. I felt something stinging my legs. I looked down: horror, my legs were black with fire ants!

Fire ants are extremely nasty little, tiny insects. They are so tiny that you don't even feel them on you, until they bite. And when they bite, they send out a signal and all of them bite at the same time. Suddenly you feel the stinging sensation. The tiny little insects leave a huge message: leave us alone or we'll bite you!

Their bites look just like the Chicken Pox. If you scratch the bites, a scar will be left there for life. A few weeks later, my son and I started counting the bites, and stopped counting at over six hundred. There were more than enough bites to do me in.

I screamed, and ran to the outside water faucet, and rinsed off all the fire ants. I knew I was in big trouble. I'm allergic to bee stings, wasp stings and - now I'm finding out - fire ant bites. Soaking wet, I ran into the kitchen, and I phoned my husband. His secretary answered, and I left a short message: "Please send my husband home, I got into fire ants." I was already having trouble talking.

The next call was to the doctor's office. I dialed - only to get their recording. I hit the" life and death" emergency choice. A triage nurse picked up my frantic call. She told me to take an antihistamine. By then, my eyesight was blurring. So, I couldn't read the labels of the bottles that were in the cupboard. I had prescription antihistamines on hand for allergies such as ragweed. In a very raspy voice, I told the nurse that I found a generic antihistamine. She said not to panic, and to calm my breathing.

I wasn't panicking; I simply was short of breath. I was having a great deal of trouble just trying to breathe. I was in anaphylactic shock. If I had known at the time that people die from ant bites when their throats close. I would've been panicking.

Sometimes ignorance is bliss.

The nurse told me that she'd call me back in five minutes. Very slowly, in my raspy voice, I told her I didn't have five minutes. I could hardly speak. I hung up the phone, turned, and became very dizzy and started to black out. I realized that I was going, and I thought, "I'm going to fall and die right here on the kitchen floor."

That's when Jesus and the Angles showed up to take me.

Guardian Angels, Guides, Spirits from the Other Side. I refer to them by all three names, but they're all one in the same. Everybody always wants to know "What do they look like?"

I found out, right in my own kitchen.

Angels clothed in light appeared from one end of the kitchen counter clear over to the sliding glass door in the family room. Each of the Angels had to be at least seven to eight feet tall. It turned out that the one standing right in front of me was Jesus. When it was "my time" He and the others came instantly.

Jesus announced, "We've come to take you."

Now, that really grabbed my attention. I didn't take the time to think about the fact that I should be thankful. Here it is "my time" and Jesus and the angels came for me. I was too busy trying to think of the reasons why I shouldn't go to the Other Side and leave just now. I wanted them to help me to survive – not die.

I didn't realize at the time, but this was the answer to my prayer. Be careful what you pray for. You might be surprised with the answer. Mine turned out to be this near-death experience.

The week before, I said a prayer asking to understand Truth, the teachings in the Bible, and what Jesus taught. I wanted to know our purpose here on Earth. You know, what are we supposed to be doing, exactly.

I wanted to know how creation works, how co-creation works, and what's on the Other Side. I wanted to understand the progression of religion over time. I wanted to know how all religions and religious teachers fit together.

Not much, mind you. I just simply wanted to get the big picture about the whole thing; everything that's out there for me to learn. I wanted to understand and learn it all. The funny thing is I actually expected an answer. Remember, "Ask, and it will be given unto you." So, Jesus and the Angels came to take me - as an answer to my prayer.

He had an easier way for me to learn the answers to these questions. He told me there was work for me to do there. He told me it would be much easier for Him to teach me on the Other Side.

I told Him I couldn't leave my husband and sons. He showed me that if I left, my husband and our boys would be just fine. He told me that our boys have "their heads screwed on right".

Well, that argument didn't work. I had to think of another reason why I shouldn't leave, and I had to think of it real quick.

Ah ha! I've got it!

When I was in Graduate School, working on my Master of Science degree, God had given me a vision that was a meditation to help others. It can help people of all ages. It helps people to be less stressed. It could help lessen heart attacks, strokes, and so on. I'd written the meditation down but hadn't published it yet.

I argued with Jesus, who was standing right in front of me, literally as though my life depended on it, and it did. I said that I had to stay to do God's work. I repeated this same statement over and over again. I have to stay to do God's work!

I won the argument.

After all, I am very convincing. My Myers Briggs ENFJ personality type is the most influential personality type, right? Aren't I supposed to be good at convincing people of whatever it is? And determined to do so?

After a very long discussion about the pros and cons of me staying here versus moving to the Other Side and working there, I seemed to convince Jesus that I truly needed to get this meditation published. I need to stay to do God's work. Besides, if He taught me all of the information that I asked to learn about, there would be someone here on this side to pass it on.

Ah ha!

He agreed that I would be taught everything I had asked to learn. I would share the information with anyone who is interested in learning it.

I didn't need to worry about those who don't want to learn, or aren't interested, or think that they know it all. There are those who don't realize that there is so much more to learn, and who don't want to listen. They want to tell others what someone else has taught them, without finding out for themselves if it's true or not.

I sat by one of these people recently on the airplane. She went on and on - I think she was trying to save me - never realizing that I have all kinds of information that I could have shared with her. I realized that even if I did attempt to share some of this information with her, that she wasn't going to listen. Her cup was full and had no room for additional information.

So, I sat there quietly. I'm not going to push my information on to anyone.

I thought I won the discussion with Jesus because I got to stay and not move on to the Other Side, at least not just yet. On the other hand, Jesus just recruited someone to learn all of this information and write about it.

Maybe Jesus won this discussion after all and not me.

This book has His information, what He wants to get out to everyone. He wants the information to reach all religions and all nationalities. He saw the opportunity to answer my prayer, and I can just see him planning exactly how to get me to happily learn the information, get it written down, and be more than happy to share it with anyone who is interested.

After all, it is my favorite subject. This was probably in His plan all along, right down to my personality type. Silly me, thinking that I, successfully convinced Him to let me stay. Jesus is the winner, no matter how you look at it.

Then, Jesus helped me to stay alive. My light bodies were put back into my physical form. It's a funny thing, I never felt dead. If someone asks me if I died, I say "No", because my light bodies never died. When you die, you're not dead. You've just simply left your physical form.

Let me repeat this: YOU NEVER DIE. You just simply leave you physical form and exist in your light body form. There's nothing to ever be afraid of about dying -as we call it.

After that, He told me to pick up the remote phone from the kitchen counter and head for the bathroom. I don't remember how I got there. Suddenly, I was standing in front of the shower. It was running. I was being told to take a cold shower.

I remember thinking, "You want me to take a cold shower? Why?"

Jesus again told me to get into the cold shower.

I took off my tee shirt discovering that not only my face and arms were red, but so was my entire upper body. I was the color of a bright red tomato, and I was covered with huge welts. I had never seen such large welts!

They were three to four inches long and one to two inches wide.

I was miserable. My head itched so badly that I couldn't stand it, and I was gasping for air. It was a miracle that I was alive and getting into the shower.

Well, I believe in miracles, and this one was happening right now.

I was hurrying as fast as I could, but it went so incredibly slow and seemed to take forever to get into the shower. I turned around, rinsed off my legs, and started to get out. Jesus told me to take more time and to use soap. I needed to do a better job of getting the acid from the ant bites off of my legs, I thought.

Wrong! I needed to be under the cold water longer. It probably saved my life.

I took what seemed to me to be a sufficient cold shower; after all, I was in anaphylactic shock at the time, and time seemed to be much different. I got out of the shower but couldn't think. I just couldn't think. I already had lost connections in my brain from lack of oxygen. So, I was told what was clean in my closet and what to put on.

I got dressed. I had trouble moving, I seemed to be more than a bit stiff. After getting dressed I grabbed my purse, the bottle of antihistamines, and my healing crystals. I figured I needed all the help I could get.

Now the problem was getting to the emergency room. I headed outside and down the driveway, bound for my next-door neighbor's house. She was a good friend and a nurse and had been an EMT. She was the perfect person to ask for help.

At the time, I seemingly went into her brain cells to ask her for a ride to the emergency room. This was a very interesting experience, because I had never gone into someone else's brain before to communicate with them. I don't believe that I ever actually called her. I'm not quite sure how she received my phone call, but by some miracle she did.

When I was halfway down the driveway when my oldest son drove up with two of his friends. They looked at me with eyes the size of saucers. "What's wrong?" they asked.

I told them ever so slowly, because it was so very hard to speak, and in a very scratchy soft voice "Ant bites."

They knew I was in big trouble. The two friends got out. I asked them - motioning a lot because it was hard to talk- to tell our neighbor that my son would take me to the emergency room.

I got into the van, and we headed for the hospital. About twenty seconds into the drive, I realized that I was about to pass out. Jesus and a dozen Angels were still there with me. They told me to aggravate my son; I told him he was driving too fast. His talking to me would keep me from passing out.

So, I insisted that my son drive the exact speed limit, and not go over it. He was going about 50 mph in a 45-mph zone, trying to save my life. He talked to me, and I was able to stay conscious for the five-minute drive to the emergency room. Another miracle!

In hindsight, we really could have used a police escort to get there faster. And we were even driving right smack in front of the police station at City Hall. Oh well.

I entered the Emergency Room and one of the nurses rushed up to get me; another nurse from the front desk asked what caused the allergic reaction. Barely being able to talk, I said "Ant bites." The nurse grabbed my hand and started hitting it to keep me conscious. She said, "Dearie, you'll be able to breathe in just a minute," and she helped me to a cubicle. Jesus and the other angels had walked beside me down the hall to the cubicle and were there.

Two other nurses ran for medications when I first came through the door. The one who helped me to the cubical stayed, told me to put on the hospital gown, and to fall over the table if I passed out; then she left to get something. Before I could get my second arm into the gown, the two returned with the needed medications, and the third returned a moment later. There we were, Jesus, 12 angels, the three nurses and me, all crowded together in this small cubicle.

I was wondering why Jesus and the Angels were still in the room with me? Were they here to comfort me? Were they here to see to it that the nurses do everything correctly to insure my survival? Were they still here in case something goes wrong and they take me?

I guess I was trying to hold onto life as tightly as I could. How do you hold onto life when you can hardly breathe? The only thing I could think to do was to hold onto my bag of crystals and appreciate the fact that Jesus was in the room with me with His left hand touching mine, and His right hand was holding my arm. Somehow, it seemed as though the only reason I could breathe was because He was there.

I was not in very good shape: still on the edge, life and death only a breath apart. I always remember that. I was lying on the bed in the cubical and I had a death grip on my healing crystals.

Life is shorter than we think. Is it ever long enough? How do we learn so much? There is so much to learn. I thought: is my life going to be cut short because I said a prayer to learn? After all, didn't I win the discussion? Aren't I going to get to stay? Do I need to worry?

No, I've already made a commitment to learn the information and pass it on. I'm safe. I'm going to make it. Aren't I? Jesus, I'm going to get to stay, right?

I saw my life flashing before my eyes. That is not only a saying, it actually is what happens. It happened to me. Jesus, the Angels, my son, and the nurses all kept me alive. I'm not in a hurry to ever have a near-death experience again.

One of the nurses put an I.V. in ever so quickly. I've never seen anybody move so fast! It was amazing how fast nurses can move when they are busy saving some- one's life. I guess that they're in their element. Boy, were they good at it.

Later, when my husband arrived at the emergency room, he stood there looking at me and couldn't be- lieve how red I was. He was afraid that I was going to die. Because of the conversation with Jesus and the Angels in our kitchen, I knew I wasn't, and they were all still there with me.

The nurses told my husband that I wasn't as red as I was before. When I was stabilized, I was sent home on medications.

I remember that my son's friends kept coming over to the sofa where I was lying down and kept checking on me to make sure that I was still breathing. My husband and boys also kept checking on me. I'd open my eyes, and there they were, standing in front of the sofa. Je- sus came and left on and off, but the other angels stayed with me. They were there watching over me.

Weeks later, when I went back to the doctor's office for a checkup, she explained to me that the cold water from the shower sent blood back into my heart to go to my brain. I did have loss of memory from lack of oxy- gen. I had problems with that for several years. It could've been far, far worse. Because of the neurolog- ical damage my doctor said that I would drag my right leg for the rest of my life.

Well, I didn't intend to drag my leg around for the rest of my life. I had work to do!

Here I go again, saying more prayers, this time for a complete recovery. You know me, pray, pray, pray; but I do it silently. Praying is not to be a thing of show; it is to be a private conversation between me and the Father, Son, and Holy Spirit. After all, what is in your heart is a prayer. So, you might know me and not be aware that I silently pray a lot.

Today I'm completely recovered.

If I had listened to the doctors - and not taken action myself to get well, I'd still be dragging my leg behind me.

That's not for me. A perfect recovery and perfect health: that's what's for me.

● ● ● ● ● ● ● ●

Before my near-death experience, I had a few visions. After the experience, Jesus came to me many times to teach me additional information that I'd requested the week before the ant bite incident. My prayer was answered. He explained many things to me that I'd never fathomed. I've been taught how to travel extensively on the Other Side. I've been given a tour of the Other Side. I've seen scenes from the future, and scenes from the past. I've been overwhelmed with the value and importance of this information. And now God also talks to me and gives me information.

This isn't a book about me. But for you to understand what I've learned, and more importantly, put that knowledge to use to make your life everything you want it to be, I have to start by telling you a little bit about my life. By outward appearances, except for what happened on 11/11, my life looks pretty normal. Take a closer look, and you'll see that I've had many different experiences in this lifetime, some normal and some not so normal. Add them up, and the result can best be summed up as my search for truth.

When I was young, I lived on a farm. It was the largest farm in the King County area in the State of Washington. My Dad was a very successful farmer. So, Mom saw to it that we had all the benefits of his success. Growing up, I was fortunate enough to take piano lessons, baton lessons, acrobat classes, and dancing lessons for jazz, ballet, tap, and toe. I went to modeling, charm, and finishing school.

Don't think we lived the life of leisure, because on a farm you grow up working hard. When I was eight years old, I started working on the conveyer belt, and then started to work on the cabbage transplanter. I rode to town to help unload the fresh produce. By the time I was ten, I started to work in the afternoon in the snack truck to replace the person who ran the snack truck but worked in the pay wagon when it was time to pay the pickers who worked in the field. I learned a lot from working the snack truck. I became quite good at math.

This was back in the days when there were real pole beans. That meant come harvest time, you needed a lot of people to pick the beans. We called them "bean pickers" and they wore worn out old jeans to work in the fields. Very interesting, now you see people out and about wearing bean picker jeans to the mall, to restaurants, and most everywhere you go. And some of these jeans are so full of holes that the jeans are indecent, and believe it or not, some of the people wearing them think it looks sexy. The bean pickers in the fields never looked quite THAT bad. I wonder what fashion will be next.

Our farm had fourteen busses to drive downtown to Seattle and Tacoma to pick up the bean pickers. They came from all walks of life. Some of our fields had pickers who had been picked up at schools. These were high school kids who wanted to earn extra money. In fact, my sister met and married someone who, years earlier had come out on a bus and picked beans when he was in high school.

Some of the fields had pickers who came literally from Skid Row. Seattle is where the term started. They were known as the "skid row bums." For a good reason: that's exactly who they were. They were not dangerous or on drugs like they might be today.

You get the idea: different fields had people from different walks of life. Dad made sure to put them in different fields. I'm sure that saved a lot of problems. I remember serving all those people when they lined up to buy food from the snack truck. I treated everyone with respect.

On the snack truck, I learned that people do what they can to survive. The bums were kind people, who were doing the best they knew how to do. I'd ask them, "What would you like to order?" and I'd look into their eyes and see many different things. I saw kindness, despair, and intelligence – or not. I'd see people out doing the best they could do that day.

So, it was easy for me to talk to them because they were just people who were out picking beans, to earn some money. They weren't someone to be afraid of. They didn't feel "entitled" like many lazy people do today.

Our family moved to Oregon when I was twelve years old. The cannery closed in Kent, so dad found a cannery near Salem Oregon and got contracts with it; Dad bought a farm near Salem. It's a very long story which I won't bore you with the entire thing. In Dec of 1970, I moved to Indiana. My parents had moved there earlier, and I was left with the family who bought our home until Christmas vacation time during my junior year. Dad and mom had planned to move back, but instead, I ended up in Indiana. I wasn't told until three days after I got to Indiana that I wasn't going back to Gervais High School, where I was a Varsity cheer leader.

Dad lost everything because of a dishonest banker who did dishonest things. Eventually it was discovered what he and his partner did. The dishonest banker went to jail for 20 years. This did not return Dad's farm and lively hood to him.

Something that I learned from this was that I'm me whether my parents are rich or poor. I'm a spirit and I trust in God.

I decided to get a job after school and on weekends.

I wound up with three, back during the era when unemployment was high, and jobs were hard to come by. I was hired as part time help, after school, at a burger place. Then, since I love clothing, I went to a dress shop and talked the owner into hiring me to work there on Saturdays and over holidays. All my nice clothing was in a closet back in Oregon. I liked to dress nicely. In the summer, after I graduated from high school, I got a day job stuffing pickles into jars. There's a point to be served by telling you how.

I walked into Miller's Dress Shop, a small shop in a small town selling upscale women's clothes. I asked if they might be interested in hiring me for Saturday and holiday work. The owner told me they didn't have any openings. I asked, "Wouldn't you like to have an occasional weekend off?" A few days later, she called back, and hired me.

I was in heaven. I love beautiful clothing. I love the styles, textures, and colors. I was a natural for working there. I could put outfits together like nobody's business. I was in my element. When school ended, that is my four weeks of summer school I graduated a year early. After I graduated is when I found the full day job working packing pickles. When cucumber season ended, so did that job. But it was time to head off to college. Then, it was hop season and I worked the graveyard shift. Then hop season ended.

It was supposed to be off to Purdue for me. But since I was just 17, Mom decided that I was too young to go away to college. So, I went to the local University and commuted from home. Since there was no money, in addition to going to class I held a job in the French lab, a job working at the University childcare center, a job being a waitress at the local hamburger joint, and on Saturdays and holidays, I worked at a dress shop.

That was enough to get me through my first year of college. Then it was off to Purdue for me.

There was always time to squeeze in a boyfriend. I always did. In the eighth grade at Salem Academy, after I finished my work early one day in Bible Study class, I wrote up a list of what I wanted in my future husband. I knew exactly what I wanted. Here was my list. The most important thing was that he would be madly in love with me and that I would also be madly in love with him. He needed to be dependable, of good character, honest, fun, intelligent, sporty- no couch potato -ambitious, good kisser (I was fourteen and had not even had my first kiss yet), like music, tall, handsome, blonde hair, blue eyes, good physique, be a good husband, wanted kids, and would be a good father. Because I read a story that their graduates would earn more money, he needed to be an Ivy Leaguer. Not that I knew exactly all of the colleges that were actually in the Ivy League. That's what I put on my list.

That, and the fact that he'd be brought right to me. I tucked this list into my Bible.

At the end of my freshman year of college, I got a fulltime job for the summer. It paid well enough that I decided to save a little bit more money before heading off to Purdue. I broke up with a very nice boyfriend in the middle of a marriage proposal, because he wasn't the right guy for me to marry. He thought I was too ambitious; this is not a good sign. Two months later, my boss brought around a new guy, introducing him to everyone in the office, including me.

The next week, my boss didn't tell me he'd invited the new guy to come up and have lunch with him. He had asked me stay in during lunch to cover the phones. I did. He headed out for lunch – right before the new guy arrived. You should've seen him scurrying out the door, looking at his watch.

Moments later, the new guy shows up, lunch in hand, looking for my boss.

You know me. I talked him into sitting at the next desk and having lunch. This was an extremely shy guy. It wasn't easy. I got him talking. All I had to do was ask him a few questions. Starting with what did he bring to eat.

We ate lunch. It took a few weeks for him to digest that. Meanwhile, I decided to postpone Purdue one more semester; after all, I was one year ahead of my age group and had taken some summer and fall night school classes. We went out. In the middle of our first date I knew that this was my future husband.

Thirty years later, we finally figured out that lunch was set up by my favorite boss. Back in Jr. High school, I made up my list, and I put out that my future husband would be brought to me. He was brought right to my desk. I must admit, I didn't expect to meet my future husband at work, and I didn't expect to meet an Ivy League graduate in a small factory in a small town in Indiana.

After all, I was headed off to a marvelous University. I never got there. We dated for a year and a half before we married.

Finally, a normal life! I got my degree, raised a family, went back to college and got a Master of Science degree.

At least until the Angels came, on November 11, 1996.

● ● ● ● ● ● ● ●

I'm happy to share the information in this book. It has helped me, and I hope you find some of it useful, too.

CHAPTER TWO

Look to Your Heart

Sometimes unexpected things happen in life and figuring out what to do is difficult. The first action to take is to talk to God and listen for His answer. He always knows the right answer, but it may not be what you want to hear. Your heart knows the right answer; so, pay attention to what your heart is telling you and trust in God.

After I married my husband, I joined the Catholic Church. I previously had been a member of the Presbyterian Church, and when my family moved to Indiana, I attended a non-denominational church where my husband and I got married. When I joined the Catholic church my husband and I were remarried in the Catholic church, since our non-Catholic church marriage was not recognized. I guess you could say we are very married. We had our 50th wedding anniversary in May 2024 and renewed our vows at a Catholic church in Germany where my husband's great, great grandfather and great grandfather had both been baptized.

After joining the Catholic church, I learned to say the rosary and have been saying four rounds of it every day. Saying the Rosary puts me into a meditative mode and helps me to listen to God and become more receptive to hearing Him. Saying the Rosary everyday does wonderful things for my life. I wake up happy, go to bed happy, and I'm living my dream! I'm so lucky to be married to the man of my dreams who God brought to me.

Another thing I have done in my search to achieve being peaceful is that I studied A Course in Miracles. It's a study course that teaches how to forgive. It also, teaches that everything you do, you do either to yourself or for yourself; that what goes around comes around.

While studying this course, I had visions. They came while I was meditating. The visions only came when God wanted to send them to me; they are a gift from God, and in His timing, not mine.

When issues come up, ask God for help, and remember to listen to His answer. Also listen to your heart. Your heart knows what is right or wrong for you.

If you ask other people for their opinion, they might give you an answer that comes from their belief system, or from something they learned from someone else, and who knows if they understand truth (understanding from God) or not. It is important for us to think for ourselves to find the correct answer, and not someone else's opinion.

Forgiveness is a key. As you forgive, you are forgiven, and peace comes to you. The first thing to accomplish is to open both your heart and mind to God. The truth is that opening your heart to God is another way of saying, "Harden not your heart.

Along with trying to spiritually improve, I decided to go back to college and get my Master of Science degree. I need to grow both spiritually and intellectually to be able to eventually advance to a higher Level. Those of us on earth are required to grow with both intelligence and the ability to love.

● ● ● ● ● ● ● ●

I promised Jesus during my near-death experience that

I would get the information out to people who are interested. That's why I'm wring this book. I've learned to forgive, and I feel peaceful. Now forgiving in general is much easier. I remember that vengeance is God's, and what someone else does goes on that person's lifeline, not mine or yours. I'm responsible for me and not for others, but I want to share what Jesus and God taught me.

CHAPTER THREE

A Visit to the Library

When I was a growing up, there was a popular picture of a Guardian Angel watching over two small children crossing a bridge. It's a picture you've probably seen, always a favorite of mine. That picture is one of my earliest childhood memories. It was always hanging on the wall in my bedroom, from as far back in time as I can remember; all the way back to the days when I slept in a crib.

I remember a time when I couldn't have been more than two years old, left upstairs in a crib with a family reunion going on downstairs. Wearing a pretty dress, ever the extrovert, even as a two-year old, I wanted to be part of the party. My mother thought differently. I cried and cried and cried, but that didn't work. Finally, after what seemed like hours, my cousin Cindy came upstairs, picked me up out of the crib, and brought me downstairs to the party.

I was so thankful for Cindy picking me up, holding me, telling me not to cry, that everything would be all right. To a two-year old she was an angel!

Cindy was more right than I ever could have imagined. When I had graduated to a bed of my own, the picture went with me. By then I knew they had a Guardian Angel, and I did, too. I'd fall asleep at night wondering what my Guardian Angels looked like.

I was four and a half when my youngest brother was born. That was when my parents decided that all four of us kids should be baptized. When my turn came, and our Minister sprinkled the holy water on my forehead, I felt an energetic sensation and I heard tones in my head that continued for hours. When we got home, I went upstairs to my bed to lie down. I knew then that the Angels would always be with me.

Months later I woke up in the morning and couldn't move my legs. After calling for Mom for a long period time, she came upstairs. While she stood in the doorway of my room, I told her that I couldn't feel or move my legs. Mom looked at me and laughed. She told me that I'd slept on my legs wrong and that they'd fallen asleep. She turned around and left me lying there.

I was alone and so very afraid. I started praying to God and my Guardian Angels. Maybe Mom had too much to do and didn't have time for me, but God and my Guardian Angels always did. I asked for them to please fix my legs. Later that afternoon, after having missed both breakfast and lunch, the feeling in my legs returned. They felt weak at first but continued to feel better until they were back to normal. I knew then that God and my Guardian Angels were watching over me, and that they'd taken care of my legs. I was so thankful.

That was the beginning of my secret private life with God and the Angels.

When I was six years old, Mom dropped me off in front of the library, telling me to open a check out card, find a book or two, and check them out. Our library seemed like an intimidating place, and I had to do this all alone in a library that I'd never been in before.

Mom wanted to visit her friend, who lived a block away, and she didn't want to arrive with two children in tow. She told me she would return when she finished visiting, taking off with my little brother, leaving me standing there alone on the sidewalk.

I was scared. I braved the seemingly long sidewalk, pulled open the large, heavy door, and entered the library.

Not knowing where to go, I found myself in an aisle with bookshelves reaching far above my head.

Suddenly a book from way up above fell on the floor right in front of me. I sat down on the floor and read the title. It was a book about Edgar Cayce. I opened the book and thumbed through it. I found it most interesting; especially since I'd already had my own experience with my legs not being able to move and having had the Angels fix them. I wondered how God and the Angels fixed my legs. I also wondered if Edgar Cayce helped people with problems like this using the information that he received from his trances.

I was hooked.

Then another book found its way to the floor in front of me from a very high shelf. It was a book about the Bermuda Triangle and about energy variances.

Wow! This was fun reading for me. It opened my mind to new and exciting information.

I checked the books out and headed out the door to wait for Mom's return. When she finally drove up, I got into the car and proudly showed her my books. She laughed at me, telling me that I'd never read books like those: they were too difficult for a six-year-old girl. They weren't from the children's side of the library. Well, even with my minimal reading skills, I read the best I could – with some help from my older sister. She was like a saint to me because she spent time teaching me how to sound out words. I skipped over some of the three syllable words if I couldn't figure them out. If my sister was around, she would tell me what the unknown word was.

I thought about how there's so much to learn about God. And how wonderful it is that books are available like Edgar Cayce's to learn about people who are doing their best to help God. How fun it was to also read about the strange things that happened in the Bermuda Triangle. The truth was I was attracted to the unusual even back then.

With four kids, a farm to help run, and a social life to keep up with, Mom was way too busy to give me much attention. But God and my Guardian Angels always had time to be with me and answer my questions. I started trying to listen to God's answers way back then. I didn't realize until years later that most people pray to God, but don't listen for the answers.

Prayer is important, and so is learning to listen for the answers. I've had a deep interest in God and the mystical all my life. I've spent a lot of time wondering how everything about God and the Universe work together.

It all started with a visit to the library.

CHAPTER FOUR

The Visions Begin

To tell you the truth, my Guides have led me on an interesting path in this lifetime. I started out just being this normal kid who was raised on a farm. My life really wasn't the same as the kids down the street; I didn't get to have a childhood until after I got married. Until then it was work, work, work.

I was always a sensitive girl. I wanted everyone to like me, even those who I now don't care a flip about. Now I know life is too short to spend it worrying about what other people think. I guess I had to get to this point to actually write this book: it's not for everyone.

I've spent my life trying to learn what the truth is about life. Because I've been searching for what that "truth" is. I've been given experiences by the Other Side to help me learn.

The Other Side is what someone might call heaven. It is the place where God, Jesus, and all Holy Spirits exist. In other words, the Other Side is not here where we mortals live; it's on a different frequency. Each of the stories I'm sharing here has a point to it. If you read them carefully, you'll figure it out.

Growing up as the daughter of a farmer was hard work. Except for my unusual experience at the library as a six-year-old, I was just too busy to get involved with anything anybody you would ever call abnormal. But there was the time I went to a slumber party and witnessed something that left me shaking like a leaf: my first contact with the Other Side.

My family had moved to Oregon. I was the new kid at the high school, and one of my ninth-grade friends invited me to a slumber party at her house along with a lot of girls who we went to school with. A party! What a blast. I wasn't about to miss that invitation.

There were more than a dozen fourteen-year old girls, sleeping over. There was lots of giggling, talking about boys and boyfriends, more giggling and even more talking about boys. That's what girls do at a Slumber party.

Then someone suggested we have a séance. I had never dreamed of being in a séance.

They explained they wanted to contact a dead person. I remember thinking, "We're going to do what? Why would we want to disturb a dead person? Isn't it supposed to be RIP?"

This was asking for trouble. What if we actually got in touch with him? If we did conjure him up, would he want to hang around? Will we bother him?

Now we're going to call on him to find out what happened to him. What if he's upset about having died? What if he's angry about the way he died? Are we safe in doing this? I was quite troubled about the whole thing.

It had gotten dark outside. We turned off the lights, and the entire party of the teenage girls gathered around the dining room table. A candle was lit, and we all held hands so there would be, a continuous circle.

One of the girls seemed to know how the thing worked: she told us to stare into the candle as she stared, asking the dead man questions. She asked very specific questions to this dead man, who was killed when he was hit by a train while crossing the railroad tracks. She wanted to know if it was an accident or if he had done this intentionally and had committed suicide.

I had no idea who she was taking about; the accident happened long before I moved to Oregon. But the rest of the girls knew all about the man. I joined in on the séance and stared at the flame for what seemed to be like an hour.

Then I saw a face in the flame!

I started shaking like a leaf. I've never shaken quite so badly. I was afraid to tell anyone that I saw the face in the flame. I slowly started asking the girls questions about the man. "Did he have dark hair?" "Did he have a dark beard?" "Did he have brown eyes?" "Did he have a strong looking face?"

Every time I described something about the face in the flame to the others, they said, "Yes, that's what he looks like!"

I can't begin to tell you how scared I was. Why was I seeing some man whom I had never met? A dead man, at that! Why didn't the others see him also?

I started asking him the question the leader of the séance wanted an answer to: was it an accident - suicide? Of course, I'd never communicated with anyone dead before, and I was not the least bit comfortable about doing something like that now. I asked him the question silently.

To my amazement, he answered my question!

He explained that when he looked down the track, the sun was in his eyes, and all he saw was bright light. I had a picture of what he saw: a very bright golden light. He thought it was sunlight. Years later, I now understand it was the golden light from the Other Side.

He never saw the train coming. He crossed the track and was hit by the train. He was taken to the Other Side, by his Guide. Now he was appearing to *me* in the flame of the candle – and I was not the least bit comfortable about the whole thing; I was extremely scared!

I never told the rest of the girls what he told me. I was afraid of what their reaction might be. I didn't understand why I was the only one who saw his face in the flame of the candle. Why didn't anyone else see him? I wondered if any of the girls who were sitting at the table had ever seen a face in the flame of the candle.

You have to remember this was my first séance. If I told the rest of the girls what the dead man told me, would they believe me? I'm the new kid in the group, and I wanted to be just the same as everybody else. I wanted to be accepted into the group as one of them. I certainly didn't want to say anything that any of the others who were sitting at the table would have a hard time believing. I decided not to tell the other girls what he had told me.

After the séance was over, we all unrolled our sleeping bags and snuggled into them. It was quite late. I lay in my sleeping bag on the floor and wondered about what had just happened. It was my first contact with the Other Side. It was all a scary mystery to me.

Later that same summer, I was invited to another slumber party. The same girl suggested that we have another séance. We all held hands in a circle again. But his time, I wasn't about to be scared – or have any contact with anybody on the Other Side!

So, I fell sound asleep during the séance. I woke up when one of the girls screamed. I left the séance and went on to bed. No more faces in the flame for me. Once was enough!

CHAPTER FIVE

My Visions

When I got home from the séance, I did tell my little brother all about what happened. He was nine. He thought the same thing that I did: the whole thing was weird but amazing. I wasn't afraid to tell him about what happened; I just had to tell someone. Little did I know that was just the start of my contact with the Other Side.

• • • • • •

Years later, I had a friend named Willie, who truly was

quite the psychic. She's on the Other Side now, but when she was here, boy, could she see the future. People would pay her to give them a reading about their future; over the years, I drove more than a few friends over to her place for a reading. She did it using Tarot Cards. When she focused on the cards, she would see pictures of the possible futures of the person who she was giving a reading for. She was able to see their lifelines.

Willie could see the future on demand. So could Nostradamus. I have tried and tried, but I've only been able to see the future in bits and pieces, and so far, not on demand. I see the pictures only when God, Jesus, or my Guides have a reason to show me something. Guess God is keeping me focused on what He wants me to experience and know.

I've wanted to go back in time to re-see some of the visions that I've had to be sure that I'm writing them down precisely. No luck there, either. The Other Side told me that I have enough information for this book. I just need to get the information out; no need to confirm the visions that I've had.

Willie and Nostradamus were psychic. I'm not psychic, at least not like them. I've been taught about the way things actually are on the Other Side. I'm receiving information dosed out to me that Jesus and God want me to know and understand. It has come in visions I've had since I turned 29, and the majority of information has been given to me since my near-death experience. Jesus has told me to share this information with those who are interested in learning about the way things really are. If it doesn't agree with what you've learned, join the club.

As far as I can tell, every church seems to think that only what they think and teach is the truth. The Catholics do this. So do the Mormons. So do the Protestants, etc. And the religions go on about who does this and who does that.

Listen to God. He knows the truth. You know those billboards that say "God Listens"? Well, the billboards need to say, "Listen to God. He knows!"

I have to keep my mind open to what I'm being taught by both Jesus and God. Since my near-death experience, they have been busy teaching me to understand the truth. I'm supposed to share what I've been taught. You may already know some of this, but maybe or maybe not all of it.

Because I've had these various visions, I now know that if Jesus or God show me something, it's going to happen - unless a concentrated effort to change status quo and create a different and improved scenario that will cause a different outcome to take place, is made. If I see it, it's going to happen. If I hear it, it might be in flux.

If we wish to change and improve the future, we, this means you, me, and everyone in between needs to change our actions and reactions from their existing patterns or habits. All of us need to work on creating a better future.

My Visions

The first visions that I had were just that: visions with movie like pictures. I didn't hear a thing. There weren't dates or a map to tell me when or show me where I was seeing something. They were simply visions that were given to me during prayer or meditation.

All that changed after my near-death experience. I needed to be able to hear what my Guides, Jesus, and God had to say to be able to receive the information I had asked for. During my near-death experience, Jesus told me I would be able to receive the information, with me being on this side. That's when this journey went into full swing. My Guides are still watching over me all the time and guiding me on a daily basis, along with both Jesus and God. Early on, Jesus taught me most of the information, but now, God has taken a more active roll in giving me information.

This book is the result of a concentrated effort of Jesus teaching me this information. I feel a great responsibility in getting this out correctly.

My first vision happened immediately after finishing a fifty-four-day Novena, during my intense Catholic phase. I was twenty-nine years old. A beautiful lady with brown hair and a huge smile was suddenly appearing to me. This was the beginning of my training under her. I asked if I could call her Kate, because I didn't know who she was, and I didn't know her name. I thought Kate sounded like a loving, strong, and powerful female name.

She became a part time Guide of mine before my near-death experience. Kate put me into heavy training in something that I call energy work. I'll tell you more about this later.

Two years later I had my first out-of-body experience. I was watching the movie, "The Diary of Ann Frank." This movie has always been incredibly scary to me. Every time I've ever watched it, starting when I was a little girl, I've had nightmares afterwards. The scariest part of the movie to me was when she was right behind the plank wall when soldiers were shinning a flashlight through the cracks in the wall to try to see if anyone was there.

I was watching it again, and I felt panicky during this scene. I went to bed and awoke in the middle of the night having that same nightmare, once again. I prayed, saying to God that I'm OK now, so would He please show me what it is that scares me so much.

The next thing I knew, I was taken out of my body by Jesus and my Guides, and the wall at the top of the bed disappeared and the entire area was now golden light. Jesus, my Guides, and I went out into the golden light. I was floating in the golden light. It felt so incredibly peaceful, I wondered if this was heaven. No, I had not crossed over to the Other Side; this was simply golden light that I was floating in. I was taken back to a past lifetime that I never knew I had.

Shocker! My previous Presbyterian and my current Catholic belief systems didn't happen to include knowledge of past lifetimes.

The next thing I knew, I was watching myself from a previous lifetime.

I was running in the rain with my husband, with enemy soldiers chasing us. We ran toward a house with plank floors on the front porch. We reached the porch, my shoes left wet footprints on the floor. We entered the house. My husband ran straight ahead to go through to the back of the house. He was going to go out the back door and get a horse to ride, to get the important papers that he had in his jacket pocket to France. I ran up the stairway and was planning to hide. I was thinking about our four children who were at home in France with my parents.

Upstairs, in the hallway, there was a secret hidden

doorway to a secret hiding place. I opened the secret door and rushed into the secret hiding place and closed the door behind me. I was so scared. My heart was pounding, and I was worried about my husband. He just had to escape the soldiers, who had guns. We had no weapons on us. We were defenseless.

Apparently, we were spies and had crossed the border into Germany. We had obtained some kind of secret information during the Hitler era, I think, and the enemy soldiers were following close behind us. Just like Ann Frank, I was now hiding from them behind the plank wall.

But unlike the movie, there were wet footprints leading to where I was hiding. One of the two soldiers followed my wet foot steps up the stairs that stopped in front of the secret door. I was trying to be ever so quiet. I was breathing so hard from running for such a long time. To my horror, the soldier took aim and shot me – through the wall.

Now I understood why the movie caused me to panic; the same thing had happened to me, people trying to look through the plank wall. But this was in a previous lifetime for me.

Anyway, I'm in quite a panic about having just been shot in the left arm. I'm looking for something to tie around my arm to stop from bleeding. Reaching to my neckline looking for a black ribbon that I often wear with one of my white blouses, I realize that I wore the other white blouse, the one without the ribbon.

I fell to the floor and died.

Now the "me" from my past, left the body that was now on the floor of the secret room, and I was hovering above the soldier. I watched my husband running through the house, from the stair railing. I watched as he was shot in the back of the head. Now we were both dead. I'm worried about the children at home. We knew at the beginning of this assignment that it was dangerous. Never in a million years did I ever think that we would die from this mission.

Then, the young soldier of perhaps 17 years old was still holding his gun outside the secret hiding place. He opened the secret door that I had been hiding behind and turned white. He was horrified. He couldn't believe that he just killed a harmless female: a female who was younger than his own mother and unarmed to boot. He was young and scared, too scared to open the door before shooting through it. He hated what had just happened.

I perceived this past lifetime by viewing it from both looking down on it from above, and also from the me in the past who was experiencing it firsthand. This was truly quite strange. How was I both here and there at the same time? I wasn't allowed to change the outcome in the past. The past was the past. Been there, done that; and learned something from it.

The purpose of having a past is to learn from it. In the present lifetime, I learned that no matter what has happened in the past, that I'm OK now. I've gained experience and knowledge from the past. I've learned to love more. We do the best we can do at the time in each progressive lifetime. Hopefully, we choose to progress, rather than regress.

It turns out that I was viewing this past lifetime from my lifeline in the Tapestry Room. That's the place on the Other Side where everyone's every thought, word, deed, feelings and emotions are recorded for all time from all lifetimes for everyone who ever exists.

Everyone has a line that goes from the past to the future. If you look to the left from the door that you are allowed to enter, you view the past. If you look to the right from this entrance door, you view the future. You must receive permission to enter this room or come with a guide. This door is guarded at all times. The guard is quite tall and is wearing white and is composed of White Light. He is kind and stern, all at the same time.

I was escorted back to my present bedroom. I saw my physical form lying next to my husband in this lifetime.

My body was all curled up into embryo position. I was floating above my body. I started to pray to Mother Mary, and a seven-year old girl came skipping towards me wearing a mid-calf length white dress with a large blue ribbon going around her waist that was tied into a fluffy bow at the back of her dress.

I wanted to follow her. I wanted to see everything that's out there in the golden light. I loved being in the golden light. It felt so good and carefree. I tried to follow the little girl who was skipping past me, but one of my Guides grabbed onto my ankles as Jesus pressed down on the small of my light body back and pushed me back into my body. I had been all stretched out trying to follow the little girl who was skipping along so sweetly. Apparently, Jesus wasn't going to allow me to explore the golden light at this time. I don't know why, but after all, Jesus is in charge and He knows what's best for me.

Suddenly I found myself pushed back into my body. I laid there contemplating what had just happened.

Re-incarnation wasn't something that the Presbyterian Church taught. Neither did the Catholic Church. I just witnessed this, and now I'm aware that I lived in a past lifetime. My belief system just experienced a huge shift. Learning the truth about things certainly requires one to keep an open mind!

God does answer our prayers, including things we're not expecting. I certainly wasn't expecting anything like this!

Now I know why *The Diary of Ann Frank* used to give me nightmares. I don't have these nightmares anymore since I now know what happened in the past, and I will leave it in the past.

When I reflect on this, I am continually amazed. How good the golden light felt; so peaceful, safe, and pleasant. I know that everything that I am now is a combination of all of my experiences, including past lifetimes.

Kuan Yin: Goddess of Compassion

One afternoon I was meditating on learning how to become more compassionate; in order to become a higher and more advanced spirit. I wanted to develop more compassion for others. I was meditating on different thoughts when Kuan Yin appeared to me.

I didn't know who she was. It turns out that she is considered to be the Goddess of Compassion. She is from a higher Level and she's helped me to become a more compassionate person. I didn't know who she was at first; I just knew that a very loving Saint (remember, I'm into extreme Catholicism at this time) who had appeared to me, who was dressed in non-American clothing.

Kuan Yin has been given the assignment of teaching compassion. She is in charge of the room on the Other Side where you go to learn how to be more compassionate. She teaches those who come to her room or pray to her to be more compassionate. People from all religions who have made it to the next Level are given assignments in areas of their expertise to help others; so we get the best of the best, and Kuan Yin is ever so compassionate!

The Serpent

After my first vision and first out of body experience, I decided to meditate and see if I could have another out of body experience on my own. Big mistake! It took many meditations before I had a second out of body experience. Finally, one afternoon while meditating, I was able to leave my body and float in light body form. I floated up, up, and up some more. I wanted to know what all was out there. Then I came to a staircase and while I was standing by a railing at the top of this staircase, another life form came and stood beside me.

It was a very tall Serpent like form, wearing a black overcoat. He looked somewhat like a crocodile who was standing upright, wearing a black raincoat, and leaning back on his tail. He suddenly started talking to me in English to my surprise and asked me to "Come with him."

I was so scared that I instantly started praying to Jesus for help. I was afraid that this Serpent would disconnect me from my physical form and that I would be dead. I was frantic. I continued to pray for help to get my light bodies back into my physical body safely and away from this evil serpent life form.

Suddenly, help arrived and protected me from the Serpent.

Thank you, Jesus. I've heard this line in movies, but when something like this happens, you truly just want to say, "Thank you, Jesus!" I was safely returned to my physical body. I was so happy to be back in my own body, and alive, that it was a very long time before I had any more out of body experiences. It took a near death experience many years later, before I was willing to have more out of body experiences.

Who was this evil Serpent? Why did he bother with little insignificant me?

It turns out that Lucifer or Satan originally came from the Serpent race. When God allowed him to tempt the human race, he and his followers were allowed to also take physical human forms. This was an evil Serpent who was not in physical form. He had nothing good intended for me. I was right to be afraid of him. He was up to no good.

The time of balancing the scale of justice is here, and

things are changing. Lucifer or Satan, the Serpent, whatever you call this evil one and his followers have been living among us. They've been living on Earth, either in physical form or else in non-physical form, as God has allowed. Satan believes that humans will follow him and not the teachings of God. You can see his evil work. It's scary. Beware of evil spirits because they do exist. By the way, not all spirits from this race are evil. Satan and his followers are evil and are up to no good! Beware!!

The Rose-Colored Floors

Back in the 80's my husband and I took a vacation to a resort in Mexico. Our suite had the most beautiful rose-colored brick floors. I absolutely loved the floors. One night before I fell asleep, I asked my Guides why I liked the floors so much and wondered where I'd seen them before. During the night, my Guides woke me up and took me out of body to the most incredible place. We headed towards what seemed to be the sun. Anyway, we went through intense yellow-gold energy to a place inside of this energy. I was worried that it would be hot and that I would burn up. It wasn't hot at all. It was just yellow gold energy. We went through the energy, like going through a rainbow, without any problems.

I started to look around, although one of my Guides was shielding my eyes so I could only look down. I could see very tall people from the knees down. They must have been twenty-five to thirty feet tall. The floors were the most beautiful shade of pink like Laurentian granite.

There were marble water fountains and marble pillars. It was the most extravagant beautiful place I'd ever been to that I was aware of.

It turns out that this immense beautiful place is where Zeus, Apollo, Athena, Aphrodite, Ares, Artemis, Demeter, Dionysus, Hephaestus, Hemes, Poseidon, Hades or Hestia, Odysseus, Heracles, the Titans, and nine Muses call home. And silly me, I thought that all of the ancient Greek stories were myths written about imaginary people. Well, that shows you what I know. Not much compared to what's out there to discover.

Recently, while meditating, Apollo appeared to me. He was wearing a yellow, orange, and purple robe with a silky-satin gold lining. He explained to me that once upon a time that they had existed here on Earth. That the same as us, they started as a speck of light, made their way through from the amoeba to humanity, advancing to human Levels One, Two, and then Three. Then they moved on up and lived on Level Four which moves you from the laws of gravitation to the laws of levitation. Then they went to Level Five to prepare for Level Six. Level Six learns how to keep Mother Earth in rotation. She is in charge of all plant life, rocks, minerals, and the elementals: which is water, air, earth, and fire.

After Level Six, they moved on to Level Seven, which assists those on Level Six like Level Four helps those of us on Levels One, Two, and Three.

After seeing this amazing place where the deities from the Greek pantheon now reside (previously from Mount Olympus) I was returned to my body and my guide pushed me back into it. I looked up, he was draped in a white robe and had shining golden light for eyes. This was one of my early spiritual experiences, so it was a really big deal to me.

At the time, the only one I could sort of tell about it, was my husband. I'm not sure exactly what he thought about it at the time, but when we returned home, I found some beautiful Laurentian pink ground granite and porcelain tiles in a shade of pink or light taupe, with black specks, that reminds me of the beautiful place I had traveled to. We had this flooring installed in about half of our home. It feels peaceful to have this flooring in our house.

Today when I see hieroglyphs of people worshiping a Sun God, I wonder if they had had an experience with those from beyond the Sun. They would have been considered to be Gods compared to us. Maybe they had also visited this beautiful place and had moved through the yellow-golden energy to get there. Native American Indians and Egyptians have interesting hieroglyphs that include the sun. I wonder what they were trying to tell us. Anyway, God is overseeing planet Earth, and Jesus is in charge of the Judgement. More about that later.

My Guardian Angel

My husband and I lived near New Orleans for four years.

This was BC; that is, before children. So of course, we went to Mardi Gras every year. One year, after the parades were over and we were walking back to our car, something quite unusual happened to me.

The street that we were walking on was closed to traffic, so everyone was walking down the middle of the street. My husband was walking on my left side. No one was to my right side. Suddenly, someone pushed me to the left. I almost lost my balance, and had to grab onto my husband, who almost fell over with me. At that very moment, a racing van sped by. If I hadn't been pushed out of the way, I would've been killed. That speeding van was way bigger than me and would have won!

There was no one there; no one to push me out of the way. At least no one from this side. I'd just had my life saved by my Guardian Angel!

An Angel from the Other Side took care of me: one of my Guides. My heart still races when I just even remember the experience. I didn't know that a Guardian Angel could physically push someone out of the way of danger. But that's exactly what happened to me, and he saved my life.

An Answer to Prayer

In 1985 our youngest son, then two, came down with a very high fever. It was winter. His fever was 104 degrees, and I didn't know what else to do. I had already given him two cool baking soda baths, and his fever was still high. It was so cold outside, that I was afraid to take him to the emergency room. I was worried that he might not survive.

While I was lying on the bed next to him, I put my hand on his forehead again to check to see if his fever had gone down. I prayed to God and asked if He would please help our son get well. I felt something strange move into my hand from our son's forehead. It moved into my hand, across my arm, down through my torso, down my legs, and out the bottom of my feet. Instantly, his fever was completely gone.

I stayed right there for another two hours. To my amazement, his temperature was completely normal. I've never had that happen before. How did it happen? I didn't know it was possible. Thank you, God: our son is well again. Early the next morning I went in to check on him: he was completely well. Another miracle!

I had so many questions about what had happened. Can that healing method ever be repeated? It all felt very strange. Was I harmed in any way? Was this simply a miraculous answer to my prayer?

Years later, I became extremely interested in energy work or healing hands. It turns out that this is a method of healing work that I apparently did in a previous lifetime, which I had no conscious memory of, especially since I had never even considered reincarnation as a remote possibility.

It is a method that can be hard on your system. I have now studied a friendlier method of energy work or healing hands. Believe it or not alternative healing really works, whether or not you believe in it.

Diseases can be energetically pulled of a person using energy hands. Viruses and bacteria are different.

There is a crystal instrument called a Cristal Baschet develop in 1952 developed by brothers François and Bernard Baschet.

When someone who has a disease listens to the Cristol Baschet being played for a period of time will recover from the disease. This instrument will not work on bacteria or infections; only on diseases.

CHAPTER SIX

The Little Voice

Ever since I can remember I've heard a little voice talking to me. When I was six years old, dropped off at the library, the Little Voice sent me down the aisle, in the library, where an Edgar Cayce book fell in front of me.

The Little Voice told me to break up with a perfectly good boyfriend because I was just about to meet the guy who I was to marry in the future, I was eighteen years old at that time. A year and a half later I did marry the new guy. I really did meet and marry the "right" guy.

When I told the Little Voice, on a first date with this guy who I met at work "I really like this guy." The little voice replied, "It's a good thing, because he's going to marry you." We married in 1974.

It's the voice of God, or Jesus, or love, or your Guardian Angels, or Guides who watch over you. All Levels, One, Two, or Three have someone watching over them from Level Four or above.

There are more Guardian Angels than we are aware of. Even the species, or otherwise known as animal life, have someone watching over them. There are even Guardian Angels watching over areas, such as towns, and countries.

Remember that the United States of America is One Nation under God. Never, ever forget that!

After my near-death experience, hearing the Little Voice became a lot easier. Jesus tutored me constantly, in order for me to be able to learn the information in this book.

It is very important for me to listen to the Little Voice, or in this case, Jesus, and hear correctly and understand what He is trying to teach me. It's important for me not to assume anything, but to be sure that I understand. It takes an open mind to learn unexpected things. I think the Bible says one thing, and when Jesus explains things in the Bible to me, I then understand the correct meaning. I'm not the only one who has mis-understood the meaning of some things, I'm in good company.

The Little Voice can also be any of a number of my Guides from Level Four, where Jesus is, and above. Kate is a part-time guide of mine, who trained me to be able to work in the White Light Room. I have other Guides who have training who help me in various things.

I have a Guide who tells me when to get up in the morn-ing, and when I need to get out of the jet bathtub that I enjoy soaking in. I have Guides who go with me when I exercise. They push me to have a very good work out. The "Little Voice" changes from one Holy Spirit on Level Four or above to another Holy Spirit. It depends on what I'm doing as to which "Little Voice" helps me. I also have Guides from higher Levels. Both Zeus and Apollo watch over me. Zeus has saved my life.

I have one Guide who must have been quite the chef. Now, when I cook, this one helps me create dishes if I ask her for help. It's amazing! Recently I have been creating the most fabulous dishes with things out of the fridge and pantry. I must admit, I do try to keep inter-esting things available to cook with. For example, sometimes I'm trying to figure out how I will cook the main dish, and the "Little Voice" who had been quite the chef while on Level Three, will start to suggest to me to get such and such out of the fridge or pantry, and to cook it in "this" order. And oh, my goodness, dinner is terrific. Cooking is more fun when I listen to the "Little Voice." My husband is now cooking too and has become quite the chef.

I tend to talk a lot. Sometimes the "Little Voice" tells me to just listen and be quiet. I can be very quiet when necessary. It's much more fun to be part of the conversation, though.

The other day, something happened that is a good example. I was out walking the stairs in Seattle with my friend. We went out to do twenty sets of the stairs. It was raining when I woke up but stopped raining. My friend and I set out at 6:15 AM, in the dark; it was wintertime. We set about going up and down the stairs, with doing push-ups at the midway point. We do pushups halfway up, and more pushups halfway down.

Well during the seventh set, my friend asked me how many sets did I think we would get in, since it was likely to rain again at any moment. I silently asked my Guides, and the answer was "Nine sets." I repeated nine sets to my friend and said to her that they have quite a sense of humor. I didn't think that they were serious about the number at the time, since it was such a strange number. Nine sets, not ten sets, or twelve sets, or fifteen sets.

As we were walking up set number seven, I asked my Guides again, silently, how many sets would we do? The answer was "Nine." I repeated nine to my friend and said that maybe we would get rained out. We were planning on doing 20 sets. So, during set number nine, it started to lightly rain. We headed to the car expecting it to rain harder. It didn't.

I drove back to the condo, and she went straight up to her condo unit. About an hour later, she called me and told me what happened when she got home. She went straight to her computer and her boss was in the middle of sending her an emergency instant message and e-mail and this was earlier than normal work hours. She was home just in time to help out with the emergency. The nine sets weren't about the gentle rain, because we would have done more sets of stairs despite the gentle rain. We quit walking the stairs because the "Little Voice" said to do nine sets.

I explained to my friend that when the "Little Voice" tells me something, that it's best for me to listen and respond. If I don't take heed of what I'm being told, then the "Little Voice" will stop giving me advice. Why should they take the time and effort to help me if I ignore them? This is really an important point, because the harder you try to listen and heed the advice, the more help you will receive.

Now, there is something really important to tell you.

Anything your Guides tell you will be from a point of love. For example, they'll NEVER give you bad advice.

Your own Yippers will definitely give you bad advice. As I explain in another chapter of this book, Yippers are made up of negative energy created from negative thoughts of your own. When you think a negative thought over and over again, it creates a thought form, and when you think the same thought again, the Yipper comes out and yips in your ear, whatever the thought is about.

People who listen to their own negative thoughts can get caught up in mind loops, or even worse, can actually hear them. When a person starts hearing their own negative thoughts, they have become schizophrenic.

You have to be very careful when learning to listen to the Little Voice. You want to be sure that you are listening to your Guides, and not your very own negative thoughts. You can ask Jesus if He is Jesus, and He will answer. If it is an evil entity, it will not give credit to Jesus, but to Satan.

CHAPTER SEVEN

SKY SPARKLES

You know what you want out of life: love, happiness, peace, fame, fortune, good health, a better life, a better job. Take your pick: you know what you want. What most of us don't know is that there's a secret to getting what you want out of life.

The secret: it's what you think.

What you think is the most important part to getting what you want out of life. Here's the reason why. The energy from our thoughts doesn't stay inside our head. It goes out to the Universe, in search of what we think we want.

That energy from our thoughts attaches to the tiny specs of

light that buzz around in the air. I call them Sky Sparkles. You can see them if you know how to look for them. I've shown them to lots of people, from good friends to perfect strangers.

Sky Sparkles are the God stuff in the air. They're specs of energy sent to us by a higher source. Their job is to help manifest what we think, and what we want. Whether we know it or not, they do their job, bringing to us what we think.

The energy that is created when we think simply attaches to the Sky Sparkles. The Sky Sparkles go out, find what we think, and bring it back to us. I call this co-creating. We are creating what we want with help from the power of Sky Sparkles.

Sky sparkles don't distinguish between our positive and negative thoughts. The Universe does not recognize the negative. If you think "I don't want", then you get what you don't want. That means you can co-create by intention deliberate positive thought or by default your negative thoughts. When you think positive thoughts, you can manifest what you want. When you think negative thoughts, you manifest what you don't want.

Think of positive thoughts as "intending." When we were kids, we did that all the time. "When I grow up,

I want to live in a big white house, and be President of the United States." Parents and teachers tell us to stop dreaming and start being practical. Most of us do. We stop thinking about what we really want and start thinking about what we can't have and worrying about what we don't want.

The problem is that negative thoughts like those don't stay inside our heads. The Sky Sparkles do their job and wind up bringing us exactly what we knew we didn't want. It isn't just being careful about what we wish for. It's also being careful and choosing what we think.

Wouldn't you rather think about what you want? Sure, you would. If you do, the Universe will work with you to help you reach your desire. It can happen in the most wonderful way, as it has in my life. I wanted a wonderful life and got it.

Think the wrong thoughts, and the Universe can also bring you exactly what you don't want. What happened to my parents is a heart wrenching example of how co-creating can work a desirable way or, depending on what your thoughts are at the time, in the most undesirable way.

• • • • • • • •

I grew up on a farm in Kent, Washington. My Dad named it Ralph's Ranch. It was the largest farm in the King County area; he farmed up to as much as 1000 acres.

Forty-four years later, his farm is no longer recognizable. My father grew up on a farm, loved farming, and was an amazing farmer. He grew all kinds of vegetables –pole beans and bush beans, broccoli, cabbage, cauliflower, corn, yellow squash, summer squash, zucchini, potatoes, fruits strawberries, raspberries, cherries nuts like filberts, and of course, he raised beef cattle.

Oh, how Dad loved his farm and his farm equipment. You know how some people love their cars, or their dogs, or their cats. Well Dad loved the land. He loved to prepare the ground for the seed, to sow the seed and watch it grow, and then loved harvesting the crops. He was always figuring how to increase the yield of his crops. Dad was the best of the best when it came to farming.

Dad had cattle, and we often named them. Since his farm was diversified, he called it Ralph's Diversified Ranch. I remember when dad was figuring out what the brand should look like. He sat at the table and doodled, scratching out ideas for the brand. He drew on scraps of paper, napkins; whatever paper was there to put his newest idea on. He eventually decided on RRD, with the first R being reversed, and the D going over the top of the second R. That was Dad's logo.

Running a diversified farm like that was a big operation. In the summer, he had 125 people on his payroll. During the picking season, there were 2,000 to 3,000 pole bean pickers working out in our fields every day. He owned 14 busses that were used to pick up the pickers. They made several runs to Seattle, Tacoma, and the surrounding areas. There were water tanks to provide water in the fields for the workers, pickups, dozens of trucks, and trailers to move the produce to the canneries, or to the conveyer belts to sort and box for fresh produce.

Oh, how Dad loved his equipment. He owned 27 tractors, a caterpillar, a backhoe, and the first two bush bean pickers on the West Coast. He invented a bean pole setting and stringing machine. He rigged up his backhoe to be self-cleaning back in the 50's.

Every Fourth of July, Dad would bring one of his big tractors with a cab over to the house and would give all the relatives a ride in the tractor cab. That took all afternoon, because there usually were somewhere between 40 to 60 people at the party. Everyone loved getting a ride in the fancy tractor cab.

Dad did a lot of nice things for other people. If someone was in need of help or money, dad was right there. He helped build our new church, bringing a crew of his men over to the church property. I remember Dad let the youth group from our church borrow 30 inner tubes to go tubing on Mt. Rainier. Boy was that fun. One inner tube was so large that five of us could all go down at once.

Our home and repair shop on the farm had everything Dad needed. He had a very large shop across the driveway from our house. The office was out there, too. There was a wood shop with all the corresponding equipment, there were two cement pits for the mechanics to use to repair the equipment, there was a tire room for spare tires and inter-tubes, and there were rows and rows of parts and tools.

Behind our back yard, we had a barn and a large pasture for Nugget and Lady, our two horses. Behind the pasture were ten more acres where Dad planted different crops. He rotated all the crops he planted in order to keep the soil rich.

Our house was built close to a bridge over the Green River. The bridge came to a T onto our road. If you weren't careful and missed the stop sign, you'd go over the edge and end up somewhere on the thirty-foot drop off to our field. Someone would miss the stop and wind up stuck in the blackberries on the hillside. It always seemed to happen somewhere between midnight and two in the morning.

Next thing you know, there would be Dad, using a tractor, pulling someone's car off the drop-off and back up to the road. Usually, they were high school kids out on a date. Last thing they wanted was to call their parents with the news they'd gone over the drop-off with the family car.

Dad would give them a polite safety talk and send them safely on their way. Dad always checked to be sure that there were no injuries. Off they'd go, never to see them again. But you knew they were very thankful.

Dad was always helping someone in one-way or another. He very often gave food to people who needed it. Dad was extremely talented and could do anything. He repaired appliances for friends and relatives. If someone needed help, Dad was there. And Dad was so kind to everyone: one of my friends nicknamed him, "Huggy Bear."

Dad was the President of Future Farmers of America; he was an Elder at church; he was Santa Clause at the Christmas programs when I was in grade school. Everybody loved my dad.

I remember my sister looking for something in the file cabinet at Dad's place a few years ago and finding his tax return from 1966. It showed that Dad had earned $66,000. In 1966, that was a lot of money! Dad owned land, and also rented a lot of farmland from others. Over the years, they bought houses and turned them into rental houses. Eventually they owned fifteen

houses, fourteen of which they used as rental proper-
ties.

As a kid, living in Kent, life was good. When you grow
up on a farm, you start working from an early age. So,
yes, we worked on the farm, and worked hard. My sister and I both came down with mononucleosis, her case
so severe they thought she had leukemia for the first
two weeks. It was from working too many long and hard
hours on the farm. But also, we had every advantage
that life had to offer. Mom saw to that.

Like Dad, Mom was always doing something for somebody. She had a big heart.

If people didn't have food, she gave them food. If
someone were getting married, she would give them a
wedding shower. She was a master organizer at giving
a party. And what a cook she was. Boy, could she cook
and bake. She was always making something for someone.

Mom had her sewing machine going constantly. If there
were a new baby coming, Mom would give a baby
shower and make a baby quilt and a baby outfit.

Fifty years later, when she passed away at nearly age
80, four hundred people showed up at the memorial
service. When it was his turn to speak, my older
brother asked, "Who has something that Mom made
and gave to them, anything from a potholder to a

quilt?" Just about everyone sitting in the church pews raised their hand.

Mom missed her calling: she should have been a politician! Mom was a red head, and definitely was energetic. I don't know how she did everything she did. She loved people and loved life. When our second baby was born three weeks early, Mom came down to Texas to help. At the same time, my husband offered to host his department Christmas party at our home. Our eight-day old son, I must admit, was the star of the party. By the end of the night, Mom knew all one hundred and twenty-five guests' names, along with all kinds of other details about them.

When I was growing up on the farm, as much as Dad loved being a farmer, Mom hated the farm life: all of the hard work and long hours all summer long. All work and no play.

When Mom met Dad, he was already a farmer. His father was a farmer. She knew what she was getting into. You would have thought that Mom would have been happy being the wife of a prosperous farmer. She was not. I can't begin to tell you how many times Mom said how much she hated living on the farm.

That didn't stop Mom from working hard. Mom did the books for the farm. In the summer, she drove the pay wagon and paid the strawberry pickers, raspberry pickers, and pole bean pickers. She made out the payroll checks. She took care of ordering the food for the snack truck. She took fresh produce, driving a large truck to the produce warehouses and helped unload the truck. On top of that, there were four children to raise. When I was three years old, Mom was Mrs. Kent. It's amazing what she could do.

She would have loved living in a house in a neighborhood up on the hill, with Dad doing anything just not farming!

Hello, Sky Sparkles!

Eventually, the farmland became too valuable, and started being bought up by all kinds of businesses. When the Kent Valley farmland started being sold and businesses like the South Center Mall and Boeing were built on the rich valley soil, Libby's cannery that the farmers had contracts with closed. They went bankrupt and didn't pay the farmers what they owed them!

Shortly before the cannery closed, one day a car pulled into our driveway. Mom was putting the garbage out. She turned around and watched as two men in suits were getting out of their car. Mom walked over to them and asked what they wanted. They explained they wanted to buy our house: they liked the location of the house and shop being between two railroad lines.

Mom told them "No way", that we were not moving.

They said they could make her an offer that she couldn't refuse. "Try me," she told them. This was in 1966, and they offered $100,000 for our home and shop!

Sold.

A deal was worked out that Mom and Dad would sell the property, but we got to use the house through the summer of 1967, the year my sister graduated from high school, and the shop until harvest season was finished in 1968. Then Dad could fade out of farming in Kent. With their other assets, there was more than enough money for Dad to retire and never farm again. Mom would finally get away from the farm.

The Sky Sparkles brought Mom an answer to her wish – a huge offer for the house and shop and an escape from a hard life on the farm.

Mom and Dad worked very hard to make the farm prosperous. They were always helping others. At the same time, Mom put her thoughts out that she didn't want to live on a farm. These thoughts manifested in a $100,000 offer for our home. That was sent from God. It was an answer to Mom's prayer for her to get off the farm.

If only the story ended here!

But it didn't. What happened next shows the power of

thinking the wrong thoughts.

Dad and Mom talked about what to do. There wouldn't be a farm for Dad, and he was too young to retire. There were four kids to put through college; I was only twelve at the time. They looked up on the East Valley hill, and found a wonderful new house to buy, that we all loved. That would have been perfect.

But Mom's cousin, who had moved to Salem, Oregon, suggested we move down there. Mom found out that the Oregon's Senator attended the Presbyterian Church there. We were Presbyterian. Mom was thrilled with the idea that we would be attending the same church as a Senator. Mom loved to be around people who she thought were important!

So, the family drove down to Oregon. Dad looked and looked at different farms. He talked to the canneries to see where he could get contracts. Instead of getting away from a life of farming that she hated, Mom wanted to move to Oregon and buy a farm. Why? Because she thought she was going to move to Oregon and socialize with the elite. To her way of thinking, that was even more important.

What was she thinking?

Dad finally found a farm, the old Borden Place in Brooks, Oregon.

The farmland was wonderful. It consisted of approximately 400-450 acres of sandy loam soil. It included thirty-two acres of Filbert trees, and ten acres of Royal Ann Cherry trees. The well pumped 450 GPM of sweet water. The farm sat on the east end of Lake Labish, and at the head of the lake stood a small dam. The Borden Place farm had number one water rights. The farm had a stately house, surrounded by magnificent oak trees. We've been told that two Governors had lived there. The property also had a second small house for the farm manager. The outbuildings consisted of a large barn, two stories tall, and a very long machine shed that housed many pieces of equipment.

In 1966 Dad bought the Borden Place farm. But Mom wanted a brand-new house. Money was plentiful, so Dad bought her a beautiful home three miles down the road from the farm.

Dad spent the next couple of years moving his operation from Washington to Oregon, all the while farming in both states. He was stretched thin, and the work demanded from us was huge. Three of us were teenagers, working until midnight and weekends during the harvest season.

Dad was the trusting type. When we lived in Kent, Mom and Dad were friends with the President of the local bank. He trusted the bankers who they did business with. Dad paid cash for the Borden Place Farm. Then, the owner of the 50 acres behind our house convinced dad to buy that piece of property. Dad had to go to the bank to borrow money since he had put everything into the Borden Place Farm.

The banker in Oregon insisted that he would only give dad a balloon note – a loan that can be called in. He had dad put up the Borden Place Farm as collateral. Dad didn't like this at all but went along with it; he trusted the banker. He should not have.

The first year, farming in Oregon started well. The crops where beautiful, but when the State Water inspector showed up, he told Dad that he couldn't take advantage of his water rights until they had been checked out by the State. Of course, Dad told him that he had bought the water rights and that everything was legal. It was.

But that didn't convince the inspector. He didn't return to give Dad permission to use the water until weeks later. Too late. Dad's crops all died on the vine. A year of lost income.

Things only got worse.

The next year, the crops were again beautiful on the vines. Shortly before harvesting time, it started to rain. And rain. And rain it did.

It rained so hard that the land became so saturated and

muddy Dad couldn't get his equipment into the fields. The crops rotted on the vines. A second year of no income.

The third year Dad needed a loan from the bank. Over the past two years, with no money coming in, investing in a new home, the fifty acres behind the home, and the Borden Place farm, he needed to borrow money to plant his crops. Dad had contracts with a local cannery to receive the crops.

The banker refused to give him a loan to buy the seeds. Worse, the banker Dad trusted was dishonest.

Ultimately Dad lost his farm. He had approximately $750,000 cash paid on Borden Place Farm.

Dad needed roughly $35,000 to buy the seed for planting. The banker would not lend him the money. The banker called the balloon note on the 50 acres behind the house. Since Dad had used the Borden Place Farm for collateral, that he had paid cash for, the banker saw his opportunity to foreclose, and sold dad's farm equipment at auction in 1970. His equipment sold for pennies on the dollar. The banker had his friend (partner in crime) purchase the equipment at these extreme discounts. Then, they re-sold Dad's equipment at market value and pocketed the difference. One example: Dad's new $20,000 corn picker was sold for under $2,000, less than the down payment. Dad still owed money on this and on some other pieces of farm equipment.

Later, the banker was arrested, tried, convicted, and sent off to jail for twenty years for what he did. I assume his partner also went to jail. But by then, it was too late. The farm had been repossessed, and Dad was out of business.

The hardest working, nicest guy you would ever want to meet had just lost everything he had spent his entire life working for. I just can't believe that anyone could intentionally ruin Dad's livelihood. Shame on the dishonest banker and his partner. How can he live with himself for doing something like that? God says, "Vengeance is mine". The banker will get demerits for this one and for all the other farmers he put out of business.

The dishonest banker is an earlier and smaller version of Bernie Madoff. It's unbelievable that anyone can steal from honest and hardworking people like that!

By the way, Dad was honorable; he paid off his debts on the equipment even though he no longer owned the equipment. If the cannery had not gone bankrupt and paid dad what they owed him, this never would have happened, so dad didn't go bankrupt, he thought it was wrong. The next year, Dad had three kids in college, since I graduated a year early. We were on our own to pay our way through college. Dad couldn't help us. I was a freshman, my older brother was a sophomore, and my older sister was a senior. We all worked very hard to get through college.

Today, you don't see people being honorable like my father anymore.

Yes, my dad was done in by a dishonest banker. But, once you understand how co-creation works, you realize it's not the whole story.

Mom hated living on the farm. That's what she kept putting out. Mom got her wish of getting rid of the farm. The Universe worked with her thoughts that attached to the Sky Sparkles, getting her off the farm not once but twice!

If Mom had realized that her thoughts would manifest with them losing everything, I'm sure she would have changed her thoughts. But she didn't understand how co-creation works through using the Sky Sparkles. If she had understood, she never would have put out that much energy into hating the farm. Mom's hate for the farm outdid Dad's great love for farming.

If Mom had appreciated what she had, instead of hating the farm, I would have a much different story to tell you today. If she had been aware of what she was doing, she could have intentionally chosen different thoughts, and had a very different life!

This story brings tears to my eyes. Dad lost the farm that he loved, and it wasn't his fault. There are many maybes that could have been done to avoid what happened. Hindsight is 20-20. I would love to own Borden Place Farm someday, in honor of my father, who loved it so very much.

There's one final chapter in this story. It's that God tries to return what has been wrongfully taken away. He did it for Dad.

Dad was a mechanical genius. He designed all sorts of farm equipment, like his beanpole stringer and setter. After Dad lost the farm, he had a vision of an invention that could have made millions. Dad drew it up and got a US and Canadian patent on his invention. But he was never able to find any investors for it.

I know the reason. Mom didn't like all of the attention Dad was getting for his great idea. To make matters worse, Mom started putting out the thought that she never again wanted anything that anyone could ever take away from her. That thought limited what could come to Mom and Dad in the future.

Most people who were once successful and fail usually succeed again. Not my Dad, due to my Mom's limiting/negative thoughts. So, when my Dad reincarnates, God will bless him with 10 times or more of the value of what had been stolen from him.

CHAPTER EIGHT

Positive Thinking: How It Works

Several years ago, I was sitting on a chaise lounge in the back yard. I prayed to gain a greater understanding of something that I was ready to learn. I opened my eyes and saw Sky Sparkles. The sparkles were everywhere. They were buzzing around like tiny shooting stars or itsy-bitsy buzzing bees.

Jesus explained that the little specs of light are energy sent from above. It's fun to see them, and oh, so easy to see them from an airplane window while traveling. I get excited when I see them and start thinking of anything and everything that I wish to manifest.

If you haven't seen Sky Sparkles yet, here's how to see them. It helps if you are relaxed, and heart centered. First squint your eyes and look up towards the sky focusing your eyes about an arm's length away. It's easiest if the sky is blue. Relax and gaze with soft vision. You'll see tiny specks of light flickering around the sky. These sparkles are everywhere, just waiting for us to use them. Intentionally using them is co-creating.

The Sky Sparkles are the basis of all creation. They attach to all thought energy and work to bring to you everything you think. What you think is the same as a prayer because what you think is what comes back to you.

Dream on; your future starts with thoughts and dreams.

The Power of Positive Thinking

Positive thinkers create exactly what they want. When things get tough, they say "Thank you for the challenge." The more loving you become in your response to everything, the more Sky Sparkles you're given to use and the more quickly you'll co-create and manifest. Perfect love reaps the reward of instant manifestation. If you don't love perfectly to create perfectly, it's a good thing that you aren't manifesting instantly.

See how it works?

Thankfulness and positive thinking can fulfill the Law of Multiplication. By thinking over and over again - positively with love you're attaching these thoughts to the

Sky Sparkles and fulfilling the Law of Multiplication. What you give thanks for, you receive more of, and if you're thinking positive thoughts then positive things multiply.

My husband started up his own business in 2001, after 30 years of a regular paycheck. I'll admit to being a little nervous. My husband's business did just fine until 9/11. After that, everything just went completely dead for months.

If he looked worried, it didn't show. He used the time to develop new products that have become huge successes. Products that might have taken years to develop had it been "business as usual." Instead of putting his energy into fear– worrying about what might happen with no income -his energy was directed into making something that would work.

There's a quote from Investor's Business Daily about success in investing and in life: "How you think is everything. Always be positive. Think success, not failure. Beware of a negative environment."

If you read the biographies of the most successful professional athletes golfer Jack Nicklaus and basketball player Bill Russell, to name two – you'll realize they did exactly the same. Their energy was directed at winning not worrying. Jack Nicklaus said he always thought that he had a huge advantage on that point. The heat of the battle would cause others to perform poorly and he knew how to handle the pressure.

Call it a head game if you want. I prefer to think of it as "removing fear and doubt." It's worked for others, and will work for you, if you let it. It's one more thing I learned from Jesus.

Here's what you do – if you're looking for more of what you want out of life.

- Decide what you want.
- Believe that it can be done.
- Picture that it has been done.

Here's one example of what I mean. Our youngest son's soccer team was in the last game of a very important qualifying tournament. The only way they could advance was to win by three goals, and the score was tied 1 to 1 late in the game.

Most of the parents had given up all hope, but not me. I was standing on the sideline saying over and over, "I know we're going to win. This is our win", and I truly believed this. A fellow parent turned and said to me, "Woman, are you crazy?"

Of course, we scored three goals in the last five minutes of the game and won the game with enough goals to advance. I never had any doubt that's exactly what would happen. It was the only outcome I could see.

You might think it's just a coincidence. You could be right, but this sort of thing has happened so many times over my life that it's clear to me it's anything but a coincidence. Keep putting energy into your preferred outcome until it's the only thing you can see happening. When it's the only thing you can see, this is what will manifest.

Saying what you want also helps. There is true power in the spoken word. When you think a thought, the process of thinking, creates energy. When you take the thought and speak it, you add additional energy to it. When it attaches to the Sky Sparkles, it attaches with a greater amount of energy to help manifest the thought more quickly. That's why, if there's something that I wish to change, I will sing about it when I'm alone. You know, when taking a jet bath, or driving the car to town, or doing the dishes or the laundry.

For some reason, winning the lottery doesn't seem work this way.

Getting What You *Don't* Want

Why do so many people worry about what they don't want?

I see it happen all the time. Somebody worries about getting sick and that's exactly what happens. Somebody worries that they won't have enough money to pay the bills and they don't. Somebody worries that the other team has just enough time left to score the winning goal.

Worrying sets up what seems to be a self-fulfilling prophecy: you get exactly what you fear. If you're lucky enough to avoid getting what you don't want, you've made yourself miserable in the process. How much fun is that?

The Cost of Negative Thinking

Negative thinkers think they're realists, being practical. Negative thinkers wonder what happened, and usually don't take responsibility for what they've created. They use excuses like "It's Gods' will."

God only loves, but *you* reap what *you* sow, so be careful: the Sky Sparkles work to bring to you what the Sky Sparkles think you want. That's whatever you're thinking. If you put energy into something, the energy is sent out, attaches to the Sky Sparkles; they find what you're thinking and bring it to you.

Pay attention to what you think, feel, and even monitor your thoughts and emotions, because what you think will be returned to you. I can't emphasize this enough!

Here are a few tips:

Put your energy into *having* what you want – not *wanting* something. Beware of wanting; wanting creates more wanting. What you give thanks for and appreciate will increase because you're putting more energy into loving or appreciating. This energy attaches to the Sky Sparkles and brings back to you more of the same.

Again, that's how you co-create. It works whether you're thinking positive or negative thoughts. You're the receiver of both the positive and the negative energy you put out. You help to create what happens to you in your life. Only think thoughts of what you wish to manifest and pray for it to manifest in a positive way. So, be very careful about what you think.

With this knowledge of how co-creation works you have a better chance of manifesting what you wish.

And there it is!

Moving Thoughts from Negative to Positive

What if you find yourself thinking a negative thought about something you don't want?

When that happens, quickly catch the thought and put it into an imaginary box and put a lid on it. When I do this, I put the miss-created thoughts into an imaginary box filled with amethyst. Amethyst purifies the energy and turns it back into Sky Sparkles to be used again. Another way to change a negative thought is to pull the thought energy back to you, rethink the thought, and then, change it to a more desirable one.

This process can also be used if you have a premonition about something that's not desirable. You can rethink or picture a different or preferable outcome. Continue to picture something better happening until this is the only thing you can see. When this new thought is the only outcome you can see, the energy has been shifted from the undesirable outcome to the preferred one.

Some people are in an abyss of negative energy. They feel hopeless, as though they'll never get out of the hole they're in. Hope is the first key to help these individuals start moving up and out of the mass of negative energy they've created. At first, in their situation, they may have difficulty feeling hope and love.

The second key is to move to appreciation: to start appreciating anything and everything they can think of. Then love will fall into place and the negative energy will start to dissolve. With work, they'll become heart centered and mellow.

Think about what you think or speak. Choose your thoughts and words carefully, because they create energy and work with the Sky Sparkles to bring to you what you think. Stay mellow. Becoming angry simply results in you thinking with less intelligence. Stay peaceful, centered, and grounded.

Hope, appreciation, and loving thoughts are the keys that'll help you move from negative thinking to positive thinking. Using these will help keep you from mind-looping over negative issues and can even help keep you from overloading on negative issues and having an emotional breakdown. There are many mentally sick people out there who've chosen their thoughts poorly. They've gone into negative thought-energy overload.

If you're depressed, start thinking hopeful thoughts. Spend more time appreciating life and appreciating everything you can think of. Spend more time sending out positive, loving thoughts, feelings, and emotions. Send forgiveness out to clean up negative thoughts, feelings, and emotions.

This approach is stress management. Psychologists will tell you that when you stay positive, you think more clearly, and negative emotions aren't clouding the brain and halting the release of serotonin from the brain. Studies have shown the frontal lobes of the brain are affected by emotional stress, and stress lessens the ability of the brain to function at its optimal level.

Prayer Works

What you think is like a prayer because it is energy being created to attach to the Sky Sparkles to bring to you what's in your heart. You get what you think!!!

The reason that prayer works is because when you pray, you are putting energy into what you want instead of worrying about what you don't want. Prayer chains work for the same reason: when more than one person is praying there's a lot of prayer energy being created. These prayers gather together to create the desired outcome. The prayers attach to the Sky Sparkles, and the Sky Sparkles go out and return with what was requested in the prayer. The more prayers said the better. Thank God as though you already have what you've asked for.

Sports

Any sport can be enhanced using positive thinking. When you think what you want to happen, you are co-creating with God, and putting out energy to help create what you desire

Cheering on the sideline is something that most fans of any sport do. There's a very easy technique to doing this: I call it positive cheering. Only cheer about what you want to happen.

For example, suppose you want your team to score a goal. What do you do? Simple: you root for your team to put the ball in the goal. You visualize your team putting the ball in the goal. You picture exactly where the ball might go into the net. You send all positive thoughts out to your team to put the ball in the goal. You picture your team making perfect passes, as this leads to the ball going into the goal. If a player from the opposing team tries to get the ball or block the ball, visualize your player out playing the opposing player. Never give the opposing team any thought-energy that'll help them to get the ball. Don't think anything on the lines of "Oh dear", or "Oh, no." Instead, think or yell positive thoughts or words like "Yes, yes", or "There you go." "Now you've got it." or "Good job."

Have you ever sat on the sideline with a parent who constantly criticized players? It's annoying. The parent who criticizes your team and figures out how the other team might score against you is putting energy into the other team doing exactly that! If you're a spectator and see a hole or weak spot on your team, simple visualize the other team not noticing, or visualize your team making a good play or move that strengthens the weak spot. Don't sit or stand there and say, "Oh the opposing team can come in and do..." You don't want to help the other team to win, and that's just what you'd be doing.

At the 2000 Olympics, Laura Wilkinson won the gold medal diving. She demonstrated a key principle in staying focused on the event at hand. She chose to stay in the now. She kept her mind in the present and simply focused on what she wanted to do. When some of the other divers had a bad round of dives, Laura Wilkinson didn't lose concentration. She wanted to dive, and that was her focus, not winning the gold medal. She didn't worry about the competitor's dives. She focused on her dives in a positive way, and she came home with the Gold Medal! The power of focusing on what you want and staying in the now to achieve it is monumental. Laura obviously focused on having a great dive, and that's exactly what she did.

Life is a Choice

Have fun creating a good life, or not, it's your choice.

Everything in life is a choice. All the decisions we make are choices. Some choices are better than other choices. The best thing to do is to make the best choice possible moment by moment. As we actively practice trying to make the best choice possible, our ability to make improved choices increases. Choices range from the thoughts we choose to think about to what we do and how we spend our time.

Choose wisely.

Moments of truth are the moments we spend choosing our thoughts, feelings, and emotions, and they lead to our success or lack thereof. Every moment of your life can be a moment of truth, because you are constantly choosing what your thoughts are and constantly co-creating your life.

If you remember the following points the next time one of your lessons in life comes up, they'll help you to choose wisely.

- Do unto others, as you'd have them do unto you. This golden rule really works.

- Everything you do, you do to yourself or for yourself. If you judge someone, you'll be judged, and if you gossip about someone, you'll be gossiped about, or if you steal, you'll be stolen from. What goes around comes around. My Aunt Laura used to say, "I have enough of my own problems to worry about theirs." This kept her out of gossiping conversations. Smart!

- Everything is a demonstration of love or a calling for love; so only respond with love. *A Course in Miracles* teaches this. When someone is nasty, they're experiencing a lack of love and need to be loved. So be nice to them. Remember to love them as Jesus loves you.

- Let go of Yippers, the negative energy that you've created. This will clear the dark negative thoughts, feelings, and emotions from your physical body.

- All things are possible with love, compassion, and forgiveness. Miracles can occur.

- Do the right thing because it's the right thing to do. This isn't always the easiest choice, but it's always the best choice.

- Only you have the power to decide if you want to be happy or angry. No one else has the power to make you angry or oppressed, except you.

-
- Two wrongs don't make a right. If someone does something unkind to you, don't do anything unkind back. Ignore the behavior. You can learn from this by deciding not to repeat the unkind behavior, ever, to anyone. Once you learn this lesson, it's unlikely you'll repeat it. That's because lessons are repeated over and over again until we learn from them. For example, once we've learned that 2+2=4, then we move on to more advanced lessons.

- Choosing to respond with unconditional love, kindness, and forgiveness, will give you continual peace. You'll feel mellow and be heart centered. Choosing to respond with kindness allows you to feel mellow, where responding with anger hardens your heart and makes you feel miserable. Forgiveness creates peacefulness. Forgiveness is the "Peace be with you".

- When someone is on the attack, disengage. Don't put any energy into responding or arguing. This separates you from the attacker and the problem.

- When we fulfill God's commandments, God fulfills His promises to us. God and teachers of God's truth want us to learn to love and forgive. When we successfully learn to love all the time with all our heart, we'll move on to the next Level, and if the next Level is Level Four, we'll walk with Jesus, Buddha, Elijah, Allah, Kuan Yin, Mother Mary, the Hindu Temple Gods, and all the others who've already made it there. If you're looking for the fountain of youth, look to your heart for loving thoughts and responses.

- Good things happen to those who do good.

- Stay heart centered.

Loving thy neighbor is to be kind, generous, and patient with others. The best choice is always to be kind, caring, and forgiving.

CHAPTER NINE

Positive Behavior

Acting "As If"

There's a bible verse that says if you act as if you have faith, faith will be given you. It's good advice, and it's an approach that's backed up by a well-known principle of human psychology, called "cognitive dissonance."

Normally, what people believe and think drives their behavior. So, for example, if someone thinks that a person who speaks slowly from the South is unintelligent then they'll treat this person as if he or she is stupid. Behavior conforms to belief. That's one reason why so many people think that attitude matters.

But the process can also work the other way. How people act can actually alter their thinking.

So, for example, if someone thinks that a slow speaking person from the South is intelligent because he or she is thinking before speaking, then they will normally act as if this person is smart. But, if they treat the slow speaking person as if he or she is intelligent even if they don't think that way, over time they will treat the slow speaking person nicer, and their attitude will change to conform to the behavior. So now the slow speaking person from the South is viewed without bias.

What the Bible tells us is if they act like they have faith, they'll wind up having faith: If you act as if you believe, then you'll start believing in whatever it is. I saw an interview Cary Grant gave. He said he acted the way he wanted to be, and eventually he became that person.

You needn't limit the application to faith. If it works for faith, it'll work in other areas of your life. For example, if you act as though you've forgiven a person who's been mean to you, eventually you'll forgive this person.

So, the next time a person is mean to you, act as if you've forgiven this person, even if you're steaming mad, and eventually you'll forgive this person.

This isn't really anything new. Remember the Bible verse that says to act as if you have faith, and faith will be given you. Forgiveness isn't any different. This agrees with the Sky Sparkle method of you receive what you think.

Practice makes perfect. You change your attitudes and beliefs when you change your behavior. This is easier said than done, but it works.

The Power of the List

I've learned why making lists work so well. When you make your list and put more and more thought energy into it, the Sky Sparkles work with you to help you manifest your thoughts.

Of course, I didn't know that until after my near-death experience, but it didn't stop me from making lists. I've always been a believer in making lists. Those lists were all about what I wanted. Not just what I wanted when I went shopping, but what I wanted for a husband, what I wanted my house to look like, the places I wanted to travel, and what kind of car I wanted to drive. The amazing thing about making up all these lists is that they always came true. It always seemed that I'd get just what I wanted. I thought I was just simply lucky.

I remember my mother laughing at some of the things on my list. But that never stopped me from putting things on lists and believing they could come true. As I think about my adult friends, my closest friends make lists, as I do, but others gave up their wish lists a long time ago. They're resigned to what they have; they think there's no point to making up any lists because they think that will only lead to more disappointments. If you make up your mind about what you really want, it doesn't have to be that way.

ADDICTIONS

Addictions are in competition with God for who or what you turn to. For example, when you feel stressed, do you turn to God and have Him help you? Do you pray or talk to God about the issue or problem? Or do you smoke a cigarette, use drugs, or go have a drink or two, or three, or more?

Do you have a gambling addiction where you might gamble away the house rent, or house note money? Do you love gambling more than God? Do you love food more than God? Do you love power more than God? We are to love God more than any addiction.

Recovering from your addiction, if you have one, is very important. When you have an addiction, no matter how good a person you are, the addiction will lower your frequency or vibration and will make it difficult for you to ascend to a higher Level. You will need a physical form to eventually move to Level Five from Level Four. So, get rid of your addictions so you can advance. You need to conquer your addiction. You can do it now, or you can do it in your next lifetime, or the next, or the next...

I have a friend who smokes. He goes outside away from others to smoke. He is the most wonderful person and does the most wonderful things for others, but he smokes. He is cooking his lungs. He is not taking care of his body. We are to take care of the body that we are inhabiting. As I'm working on this 5th edition, here's an update; he has passed on from smoking. He tried to quit but could not. He is now on the Other Side. We miss him. It's so unfortunate!

We are commanded to love God and have no other Gods before him, such as an addiction.

When Others Behave Badly

If everyone took the time to be kind to others we'd be living in a very different world. Caring and kindness are the keys to loving thy neighbor. But sometimes our neighbor can be difficult, like when they display undesirable behaviors. What do you do then?

One way is to think, "Oh, they're doing that again." Another way is to simply look at the big picture and think to yourself, "I don't want to play that game anymore." Then get on with your life without judging the other person. Simply allow the other person to learn and experience and practice their lesson.

It's OK for you to choose to live in a better reality, filled with happiness, love, and compassion. Since you've already learned the lesson the person is choosing to experience, at some time in this life or another lifetime, you've been there and done that. Let the other person learn and move on with your own lessons.

Do that and you're learning your own lessons and allowing your neighbors to learn their own lessons. Remember to be kind to your neighbors when they're learning lessons that you've already accomplished learning. We learn at different rates and at different times. Sometimes it's so obvious to us what the right answer is for our neighbor, but we need to allow our neighbor to learn at their own rate. Avoid the temptations of worrying about when your neighbor will learn a lesson. Keep your focus on what you're trying to learn, your lesson at hand. You're only responsible for you.

When it comes to choosing your friends, pick them very carefully. Don't hang around negative, toxic people. Choose people who have positive thoughts and who try to always do the right thing. Those who are not trying to improve aren't evolving into a better person, but stagnating. Those who are always trying to do the right thing are on a positive path. They'll succeed getting to the next Level, and the next.

We're all here trying to get to the next Level, no matter what Level we're on right now. There's always the next Level to get to: use the Sky Sparkles in a positive way to help you to get to there.

CHAPTER TEN

Forgive and Move On

I'm sure you've noticed that the older you get the harder it is to remember things. When we were young, we never had any problems with our memory. Now, it takes hard work to remember the places where we've been and the names of all the people we know. Maybe that's because our brains are like computer memory; the more you have stored up there, the more there is to sort through. That sorting takes time. To say nothing about all the things we've forgotten along the way.

So why is it that we have perfect recall of every single thing that every single person has ever done to us that we thought was wrong? Those memories never fade with time. Thirty years later, we're still steamed over something that somebody did in high school. That we remember like it happened yesterday. It's as if all the hurts get stored in a special part of our brain. It's made a good business for book publishers and psychiatrists. We know life will give us some tough shots, and not everyone will always be nice to us.

That's a 100% guarantee. So, what are your choices? You can be mad, and carry that around with you, and every time it comes up, be miserable all over again. Doing that gives huge power to that other person and they probably don't even remember what they did in the first place. Even if they do, you're still the one stuck being upset.

Revenge makes for a great movie, but normally, it's impractical. Besides, plotting revenge requires putting even more energy into something that happened in the past. If you hold grudges against others, you're really just holding them against yourself.

You could try to just forget about it. That would work if only you could just tell yourself to forget the whole thing, just let it go. The problem is that you can't do that; your brain just won't let you. More likely, you'll wind up in a mind loop over these issues. Mind looping is when you recycle the same thought over and over again.

Emotions can play havoc with your health. When you're experiencing emotions that are not peaceful, happy, or you're upset about an issue or another person's behavior, you're putting out negative or black energy. That creates more undesirable negative energy.

Negative emotions can cause diseases such as cancer, leukemia, lupus or any other disease that you can think of. People who get diseases and then go into remission have successfully changed their thoughts so that they're no longer putting energy into the undesirable issue at hand.

Yes, you're responsible for your health!!! Don't blame it on God's will. God doesn't will you to feel anything except love, peace, joy, and contentment. He doesn't put the black energy around your body that sinks into your physical form to put your body on overload and end up with a disease. You do that all by yourself. When you get too stressed, you put negative black energy out that not only goes out to be returned to you, but also surrounds your own physical form.

Dr. Bruce Lipton has done incredible research on how our DNA releases chromosomes responding to its environment. Hence the hereditary factor is really the thought pattern that we might be repeating from our relatives, which creates a certain environment for the DNA in our bodies to release particular chromosomes, which may result in what we presently call hereditary diseases. Break the pattern and avoid the disease. It's not God's will for anyone to die of cancer, or any disease for that matter. Change your thoughts to thoughts of love. Let go of all anger or negative thoughts to live a happier and healthier life.

Healing

One day when I came out of the grocery store, I found a scratch of peach colored paper with a Bible verse on it. This piece of paper was stuck to the edge of my car window. The Bible verse was Psalms 1.19:11.

As I read the piece of paper, I thought that one of my Guardian Angels put it there for me. I'd been meditating on how to move my most hurtful past issues into unconditional love. I'd been praying for help on how to move these past hurtful issues, and here was my answer.

I went home and looked up the verse before putting all the groceries away. The verse says, "Thy word have I hid in mine heart, that I might not sin against thee." OK, here it is. It's so simple, as everything is with God. I am to keep love in my heart at all times. If you're experiencing love, then you're not experiencing hate or anger. God's commandment is to love with all our heart, mind, soul, and strength. This becomes much easier if we're not busy being angry.

Sin, or self-inflicted nonsense, is a result of not keeping love in our hearts. How simple God's law of love is, and how complicated we seem to make it. If we are busy being heart-centered and mellow, then we are not hardening our hearts and spending our time being angry or feeling hurt.

I've heard people complaining about "needing to heal." That means they feel like they're a victim. Don't make yourself a victim.

For example, if you had a problem with your father or mother and can't quite bring yourself to forgive them or "heal" then realize that you are actually not forgiving yourself from some lifetime or another. Think to yourself. Who knows when I might have done such a thing, but now it's time for me to let go and move on, I'm healed of my own folly. I have control of my happiness or sadness.

All you have to do to heal yourself is choose, to forgive the other person. Sometimes we forget to keep love in our hearts. Instead, we choose to feel hurt. That's our choice: it's up to us to forgive them. When you choose to forgive, you're in control of your choices and your life. When you forgive the other person, you've also forgiven yourself. Then you can move on to your next lesson.

The Next Time It Happens

Now you have chance to practice using this wisdom the next time someone displays some unkind behavior to you.

It's possible they don't even know what the lesson is in the first place. The person may not even get that they've committed an undesirable behavior that has been unkind or rude, or mean.

If the person had followed the Golden Rule, "Do unto others as you would have them do unto you," they wouldn't have displayed the behavior in the first place.

Next, simply forgive the person. It's their problem – not yours. But you don't want to give any positive reinforcement for undesirable behaviors. While forgiving is always the right thing to do, don't do anything to further encourage the behavior, and don't forget what you just experienced or learned.

Sooner or later the person might figure out that they've been unkind and apologize. That means they learned something. Hopefully, they won't continue to display that behavior in the future.

It's a good idea to pay careful attention to the behaviors of those who you consider to be your friends. It's very possible that the person may be running a pattern of this negative behavior, which means they're likely to repeat the behavior. No need to be there and give them the opportunity to do that to you, again.

Life is too short.

If a friend is lacking in character, the best thing to do is to back away from the friendship. There are so many wonderful people in life. Spend your time with them and leave the other kind of "friends" in the past. None of us need a friend who is actually a "frenemy" in our lives.

Yippers

When you become angry or upset over something, you create negative thoughts that hang around you. You're the one carrying around that negative thought: they're your creation, and they belong to you. When you think the same negative thought over and over again, it actually creates a thought form. I call that a Yipper. A Yipper is a black, toxic, negative thought form. It looks like a Gumby: a tall and narrow stick person with no arms or legs.

This negative thought form can attach itself to an area of your body, or an organ in your body. Your body responds, and it becomes sore or sick. This is your body's way of telling you that you need to re-choose your thought. It's telling you that you have a negative thought form hanging around you, and that you need to get rid of it. Sometimes people go into surgery and have some part of their body removed. Actually, the person could have kept whatever body part was removed if they had re-chosen their thought and exchanged it out for a different and more peaceful thought.

This thought form comes out to yip at you each time you revisit this negative thought. Every time you do, the Yipper grows. When it gets large, instead of thinking or mind looping, you may actually hear the thought form yip at you.

When someone goes from thinking the negative thought to hearing the negative thought, they may think that God told them this negative thought. That result is Schizophrenia: they've been overcome with the negative energy of this thought form. God doesn't tell anyone negative thoughts, such as telling them to commit suicide. Yippers do this, not God.

There was a mom in the Clear Lake area that drowned her own children in the bathtub because she said that God told her to do it. This mother was listening to her own negative thoughts, not to God. God would never tell a mother to drown her own children. A person who can't differentiate between their own negative thoughts or Yippers that they're mind looping on, and believe that God is speaking to them, is displaying schizophrenic behaviors. There are those who can differentiate between the Little Voice of their Guides and God, and there are those who mind loop on their own Yippers, that they've created all by themselves. Most people can distinguish between them.

You've heard the saying "The devil made me do it"? People think these thought forms come from the devil. They don't realize that they created the thought form all by themselves.

One way to help you know who you're listening to is to ask the question "Is this from the Voice of Love?" or "Is this from a source of love?" If you're not hearing thoughts from a loving source, then it's possible that you're listening to your own negative thoughts, or Yippers, that have come out to yip at you.

The best answer is to "Get over it." as my best friend says. In other words, forgive in order to get rid of the Yipper - or keep from creating one in the first place.

Forgiveness ends mind looping. Forgiveness can help diffuse an existing Yipper. Forgiveness releases the black toxic negative energy. It shrinks the Yipper. Forgiveness sends out White Light to dissolve the black toxic energy of the Yipper. Once you've forgiven, you've passed the test and have learned whatever the test was about. Forgiveness equals success.

Forgiveness Is The Answer

Once, when I was thinking about one of my Yippers, the next thing I knew I heard Jesus telling me "As I forgive, I am forgiven." This is in the Lord's Prayer. Forgiveness is the answer.

Forgiveness is using my energy to create my best option. I find a different way of looking at the situation. I forgive myself for similar mistakes I may have made in the past, or in one lifetime or another that I don't remember. The problem I have with them may be a reflection of my own weakness that I see in the other person. I have the opportunity to make an adjustment to be in balance.

When I forgive others, I'm demonstrating the fact that I've learned not to do what they did. If they knew not to do whatever it is, they wouldn't have done it. Or possibly they knew it was wrong and thought they could get away with it. Obviously, there is a lack of understanding that there are consequences for the action or behavior. Consequences are demerits given out during one stage of the judgment period.

I've recently had a huge test on forgiveness. I went through the process of forgiving. I remembered that God says that judgement is His, and as I forgive, I am forgiven. So, I gave the evil deed that was done, to God, and instantly peace flowed through me. I find that forgiving those who have done unkind things to me makes my life peaceful. I wake up happy and I go to bed happy.

The more practice I have forgiving, the easier it becomes. It's like you get the hang of it, like riding a bicycle.

CHAPTER ELEVEN

The Answer to My Prayer

Just before my near-death experience, I prayed to be able to understand why we're here on Earth, how creation works, and where are we headed after we die. The answers came faster than I ever expected, and I got them in a way I didn't want, by almost dying. A word to the wise: be careful what you pray for.

But the answers did come; my prayer was answered.

First, I want to tell you how kind Jesus has been to me. I can see how much love He has become, and I'm a so much smaller amount. He treats me as though I've already earned the status of Level Four (shortly, you'll know what that means). The truth is, in comparison to

Jesus, I feel like a peon. Jesus has told me over and over again that I'm taking this too seriously. His way of getting me to lighten up is to wink at me. Then I smile, laugh, and relax, then I am less intimidated, and it is easier for me to grasp what He is saying.

So, now I know the answers to those questions. And I've learned a lot of other things about what happens on the Other Side. I didn't want to die, so I negotiated a deal to get to stay on this side: my commitment was to share everything that I would learn with those who are interested. Here's what Jesus has explained to me about how the path of creation works.

It's all so simple.

● ● ● ● ●

Jesus wants us to become greater and greater amounts of love. He wants us to do what he did. He wants us to increase the amount of love in our hearts and become pure love. He wants us to learn to forgive unconditionally and be peaceful.

Our planet is set up so that our spirits advance or regress according to how much love we are at the end of our lives. As love grows and develops, it goes from a less advanced species to a more advanced species. Without becoming more love, there is no advancement.

During our life, we grow in both love and intelligence. But unlike other planets, at the end of our life we advance by the amount of love we have become, rather than by the amount of intelligence or consciousness we have gained. Because of that, spirits on Earth are advancing faster than any of those from other planets. That's because the energy of love is a higher energy than that of intelligence or consciousness.

For centuries, God has sent teachers to all religions. Krishna, for example, was thought to be the 8th incarnation of Vishnu. It is said that he disappeared from the earth, and most likely ascended in physical form to Level Four.

When my husband and I visited Athens, I heard about Zoroaster and Athena. Zoroaster was credited with defeating the evil one, Angra Mainyu. Zoroaster was also associated with Nimrod the Babylonian who invented astrology. Athena was known as the patron Goddess of Athens.

Confucius taught not to impose on others what you do not wish for yourself. This was long before the Golden Rule in everything, do unto others what you would have them do unto you. Remember that what goes around comes around, or as described in The Course in Miracles, everything you do, you do either to yourself or for yourself.

Buddha was another teacher sent by God before He sent Jesus. He wrote the Four Noble Truths, which became the tenets of Buddhism.

As we become ready to learn the next step, God has sent teacher after teacher to teach us more advanced spiritual lessons. He's sent teachers to every religion, and to every part of the world. These teachers have taught lessons of love and gratitude. They have been depicted through time as Angels with wings to denote that they move by the laws of levitation and are from heaven. The ancient Egyptians in their hieroglyphs denoted those who move by the laws of levitation as having bird heads. We may call the Level Four spirits our Guides, Guardian Angels, or Angels.

After these teachers, God sent Jesus Christ. He is called The Lamb of God and is in charge of the Judgement. Matthew, Mark, Luke, and John wrote accounts about His life that are in the Bible. Jesus ascended in physical form to Level Four.

He came to teach us about forgiveness and eternal life. Jesus had the most difficult job of all. He came to teach people to love thy neighbor unconditionally and teach that life is eternal.

• • • • • • • •

Now to explain the Levels.

God created energy and it went into the amoeba, and the energy grew in consciousness and love. As the spirit grew in love and consciousness, the spirit moves up through the species. When the spirit reaches a sufficient amount of love to become human, the spirit will be born as a human being, Level One.

As we grow in love and open our hearts and minds to God's love, we move up through three levels. If we only have enough love to be a Level One or Level Two, we make more mistakes than Level Threes because we haven't learned as much just yet. Because we might make big mistakes, we aren't given as much energy to co-create with. As we grow and open our hearts and minds to listen to God, we receive more of God's energy to use. As a Level Three, we're more likely to use God's energy wisely, than a Level One or a Level Two.

Level One people have just come across from the animal species unless they regressed from Level Two. Level Ones are usually concerned with survival. They would prefer for you to take care of them, so that they don't have to spiritually evolve. If they had their way, they would be happy to regress. They don't yet understand what they're supposed to be doing. They tend to be slothful and lazy.

They're here to learn not to steal, not to lie, not to cheat, or be greedy; not to kill other humans, not to commit adultery, etc. You know the list: it's in the Ten Commandments. They don't understand that what goes around comes around. They want entitlements. They don't understand that they need to be responsible for themselves.

A Level Two has more love and thinks differently than a Level One. But they are immature: they don't see the big picture just yet. A Level Two believes that he or she is smarter than their parents. They're like the teenager who thinks they know it all, but they don't. Actually, they have a partial picture of what's going on. They're closed; their hearts and minds have not yet opened to God.

Level Twos think they know what is good for you and try to force it on you, whether or not you want it. They don't understand that God has given us free will. They like Socialism, and even Marxism, or worse yet, dictatorship. They try to control others when they can't even control themselves. They want to take what one person has and give it to someone else - so that they will feel better about themselves.

What a Level Two doesn't get is that if they steal from others, they are truly only stealing from themselves. That's because the Fairness Master is watching and will debit them seven times of the amount sooner or later, this life or the next.

They're avoiding learning the blessings of God's laws. Level Twos who have managed to become rich, are often greedy, and only use their money selfishly, and spend much of their time worrying about their money.

They don't learn the Law of Multiplication through generosity. Worse, they may have made their money in illegal or unethical ways. They don't know that somewhere down the line, their illegally gained money will be lost, either during their lifetime, or when they reincarnate. Level Two's get jealous of those who work hard and earn a good income.

A Level Three has more of the energy of love. Their hearts and minds have opened to God. They're trying to follow God's laws and not be greedy, or steal, or cheat others. They're self-reliant. They're generous. They're very adamant about being fair. They understand fairness and they want to help others in whatever way they're suited to do so.

A Level Three allows others to develop at their own rate. They know that God gave us free will and allows others to use their free will. Threes take care of themselves, and silently help others.

Satan and his followers have been reincarnating into human form. They're lower than Level One. If you look carefully, you can see who some of them are. They like to get into positions of power and try to control the rest of us, tell us what they think is good for us. If they manage to get rich, they don't donate to help others. They're all for taxing others, but cheat on their own taxes. They want to redistribute the wealth by taking it from hard working people and giving it to those who have not earned it. This is stealing! They cheat, are greedy, and tell lies.

They think they're smarter than the rest of us. The truth is, they aren't smarter than the rest of us, and they don't understand the Fairness Master. Life over, when a person dies, they are the amount of love they've become during their lifetime.

When I was trying to understand this evolution of the spirit, I was shown what happens to a hateful person who died. First, the negative energy was separated from the love. What was left was how much love they were. Then, the negative, black, toxic energy was purified with love, or White Light, and sent back into creation as Sky Sparkles to be used again. The love that was left from their spirit was temporarily immersed in the Golden Light of love.

The spirit was then sent back into the process of creation, to the Level of love that had been attained, to reincarnate to continue experiencing, practicing and learning. That might be a Level One, Two, or Three. If there's not enough love left to stay on the human Level, the spirit will go back to a lower species. It might be reincarnated as a fish, a bird, a cat, a dog, or whatever animal matches the amount of love attained during the lifetime.

In other words, this spirit flunked out of the human race and was put back into the developing creative process. This spirit will make it back to the human Level someday and eventually, hopefully, continue.

We attain the level of love we choose to become through our thoughts, feelings, emotions, deeds, and choices. That determines the amount of love we are in our hearts. God gave us free will to choose when we become a greater amount of love.

A developing spirit will continue on the path of both a greater amount of love and consciousness as it progresses up through multiple lifetimes. When a spirit crosses over and has reached Level Three, the spirit will be escorted to the White Light Room for Level Three and will be given a period of three days to "Move through their heart" with love. Then the spirit, not in physical form, will move to Level Four and be initiated into the Assembly of the First Born by Jesus.

"Crossing over to the Other Side" is just another way of saying that someone has died and has taken the White Light tunnel to the White Light room.

Being "Born again" happens when a person has moved to Level Four with a physical form by becoming perfect love or giving up his/her life to save another. Jesus then initiates the ascending person into the Assembly of the First Born.

This is our purpose in life while here on Earth; to be initiated into Level Four with a physical form, to the Assembly of the First Born.

CHAPTER TWELVE

The Process

As you can see, we clearly are evolving, starting from the speck of light or breath of God that became life, as mentioned earlier. When God creates this energy, He becomes responsible for what He creates. He also set up a system for us to grow and learn, essentially cause and effect. We learn by trial and error. What works for us, we repeat. What doesn't work for us, we will discard sooner or later. Sometimes it takes a life changing experience or a life crisis to let go.

We're here learning to become loving spirits to become the master of love. When we master being a loving person, we'll dissolve the darkness that we individually have created. God doesn't cause our negative thoughts, feelings, or emotions, or choose our wrong choices. We do that all by ourselves. We've been given free will to choose when to learn. God waits for us to experience life and to learn through our experiences. When we learn one thing, we continue on to learn more advanced things. This is how it's been on Planet Earth throughout the ages.

Since we are born without complete knowledge we must live, practice and experience to learn. Every so often someone makes the statement that we are "born into sin." You've heard this statement, haven't you? We are created to become perfect love, and this takes lots of experience, practice, and learning. **We are born to learn and spiritually advance. Think positive!**

Since we learn through experience, in one lifetime or another we've done most things either by experience or by watching others. We have become the product of our experiences and what we have learned. This is one reason that we're not to judge others. At some time or another we've "been there and done that or learned that". We've learned and we need to allow others to learn. Life is a choice.

Sooner or later, we'll learn whatever is out there for us to learn. Most of us continue on an upward spiral. Some insist on choosing a negative or downward spiral. Pray for mercy for them.

If You Haven't Earned It, You Don't Deserve It

Once you open your heart and mind to God, you will take on the same beliefs a Level Four has. You'll believe in fairness, which is that you deserve what you have earned, and only what you've earned.

There are no free lunches! It takes hard work to achieve something. You don't get to the next Level by taking a free ride. You get there through self-improvement. This is done by working and earning your own way. You earn it; you don't inherit it through other peoples' efforts.

This is all part of spiritual evolution. Our spiritual evolution happens whether or not we make the best choices. Either we learn the easy way, or we learn the hard way. It's our choice.

We're all here to advance to the next Level. Those who have made it to Level Three have opened their hearts and/or minds to God. They are influenced by Level Four. They understand that they only deserve what they earn, and socialism programs slow us down, make us lazy, and can cause us to lose ground and spiritually regress.

You become a responsible person; you work and earn what you have. You make your choices. First take care of necessities, and then you can indulge in luxuries. You are responsible for your own success or lack thereof. It is not beneficial to redistribute income from responsible people to irresponsible people.

The sooner you evolve to a higher Level, the happier you'll become. Those who wallow in their problems create more problems for themselves. Those who pick themselves up by their bootstraps so to speak, and get to work, improve their life situation. In doing this they're also spiritually evolving. Again, it is cause and effect in action. Good action receives positive reinforcement, like a paycheck! After all, good things happen to those who are good people, who deserve something good.

We're here, doing what we're doing and experiencing what we choose to experience. The end result is that all of us will continue to grow in consciousness and love from the point where we are. Sooner or later, we'll all get to the next Level. Our potential is unlimited; we'll amaze even ourselves.

Level Four - and Beyond

As we grow in both love and consciousness, we move up through the three human Levels. When we become perfect love, we'll move to Level Four in physical form. This will happen individually, as each of us becomes perfect love, and learn to forgive perfectly. Perfect forgiveness is unconditional love. Unconditional love is perfect love. We have eternity to accomplish this.

Diligently seeking God and being kind and caring of all others, unconditional love, is what is necessary to ascend to Level Four.

What happens when you master becoming perfect love is this:

First your heart will send a message to your brain that you have achieved loving others to a sufficient amount required for you to move to Level Four. In other words, you have mastered loving thy neighbor.

Your heart will send a message to your pineal gland, which is a gland in the middle of the top of your head in the middle of your brain, to open fully to receive a greater amount of Gods' energy to use and co-create with. This will look like the picture of Jesus in the Garden of Gethsemane. At the same time, a message will be sent to your gallbladder to start functioning. Your gallbladder will now manufacture all needed minerals for your body to stop aging. When this happens, you can maintain a youthful, healthy body for eternity. This is how Jesus is in the same body 2000+ years later. Your heart is your very own fountain of youth. When this happens, the spirit has been "Born again" and Jesus will then initiate this spirit who has become the embodiment of Love, and this spirit will now have a physical body on Level Four that will be under the laws of levitation instead of the laws of gravitation. Jesus is the one who Initiates the "Born again" spirit and that is why He said, "You cannot get there but by me."

Let me explain. Jesus died on the cross to forgive our

sins. If we move through our heart with love during the three days that we have in the White Light Room Level Three, after we die, Jesus takes us to Level Four and Initiates us into The Assembly of the First Born, Level Four even though we haven't earned it! This is the GRACE of God. A Level Three spirit, who has not become the embodiment of perfect love, will be initiated into Level Four without a physical body.

This grace is not given to Level One or Level two because their hearts and minds are not open to God. You must have your heart and mind open to God to reach Level Three.

After Jesus initiates a Level Three into the Initiation Room, the initiate is sent to a room located just outside the front double doors, to the right, as you exit the Assembly of the First Born or, as I call it, the Initiation Room. This is where the Initiate will receive additional training. After the Initiation, the Initiate will be given an assignment; either to help others in something the Initiate excels in, or be given an assignment to help another in an area that the Initiate is weak in.

CHAPTER THIRTEEN

The White Light

After my near-death experience, I'd been in training on the Other Side with Kate. She's the one who appeared to me after I finished a fifty-four-day Novena, when I was twenty-nine. Kate is from the highest Level. She gave me permission to call her Kate, as I've stated before. I'm told that I'm named after her. My name is Nancy and is a simple variation of her name.

She is a part-time Guide of mine.

She's been teaching me incredible things. I pray and ask to learn many things; she teaches me, and I listen and learn. I've had to greatly improve my listening skills. Since my near-death experience, I've done much better. I listen better and it's much easier to do out of body travel. Now I feel safe whenever I travel out of body. My Guides are always with me.

Kate taught me how to separate darkness from light in the White Light Room. My training started because I wanted to explain to people who made it to the White Light Room what it is, and what they're supposed to do when they get there. I figured if I didn't know, I would appreciate someone explaining it to me.

Prior to my volunteering, many deceased Level Three spirits never figured out what they were supposed to do during their three days in the White Light Room. They sat there alone for three days being depressed about the fact that they'd died. Needless to say, only a few ever made it to Level Four. Now just about everyone who's made it to the White Light Room in Level Three is initiated into the Assembly of the First Born.

It's amazing how much it helps to give simple instructions. I just wanted to help people who cross over. I wanted to give them the kind of help that I would appreciate receiving if I'd found myself in their shoes.

I hadn't finished being trained when Dad died.

I can't explain how devastated I felt. You see, when I was a little girl, I was Dads' little "Blondie." I would rub my Dad's back, and then he would pick me up and sit me on his knee. For me, this was a big deal because Mom was too busy with whatever it was to pick me up.

I wanted Dad to make it to Level Four instead of dying and reincarnating as a Level Three. I wanted him to be Initiated by Jesus. If that didn't happen, I thought I had failed. I didn't work hard enough or fast enough or something. The truth be known, I'm only responsible for myself, and Dad is responsible for himself. But that's not how I felt at the time of his death.

So, when Dad died, I prayed and asked if I could enter the White Light Room where he had been taken to by his Guides. I was given permission and taken there by Kate.

She took me into the White Light Room where Dad had been taken. I asked permission if I could send the White Light onto him to try to eliminate any traces of toxic energy that was surrounding him. The answer was yes.

I stood there and sent a thin stream of light from my heart, as much White Light as I possibly could at the time. While I was doing my best, Kate sent a huge stream of light that instantly took all the toxic energy away from around Dad. (Now, at this point of my life, as I'm making this 5th edition of this book, I can now do that, and I can now help others whom I'm allowed to help on the Other Side).

We're only allowed to help to the point of the darkness being gone, because the spirit in the room must open or push through their own heart with love by them-selves. No one can do this for them.

I talked to Dad about his good memories until he moved

through his heart with love. Instantly, Jesus was standing there in front of him and took him through the door into the Initiation Room. Dad was then Initiated into the Assembly of the First Born. My Dad made it to Level Four! It was different than I'd ever imagined, I was invited to witness his Initiation. Those who make it to Level Four without a physical body will eventually reincarnate to get a physical form Ascend in. We cannot move on to Level Five without a physical body.

After being initiated, Dad was sent to take classes that would teach him a few more things that he would need to know. Dad was given his Level Four assignments.

One more thing about Dad, he had good character. I considered Dad to be like a saint. He didn't drink, smoke, swear, or have any addictions. He only said kind things about everyone.

Later, when a very dear friend of our family died, I asked for permission to help him. By then, I'd grown much stronger at sending the stream of White Light, so I was able to do this without help from Kate. I entered the White Light Room and greeted my friend. He asked me what I was doing there.

I explained I was there, as a volunteer and I wanted to help him. I told him how I could do that. Then I sent the stream of White Light to him to clear the dark energy that was surrounding him caused by his negative thoughts, feelings, and emotions. The next thing I knew, he was clear of any negative energy, but he was shorter than before. He said to me, "Nancy girl, what did you do? You shrunk me!"

I had to explain to him that shrinking happens when you separate the light from the darkness. You keep the light and get rid of the darkness. You're the amount of light that's left. In his case, after removing the darkness from the light, he was a little shorter. When this happened to Dad, he was approximately the same size.

My friend and I talked for a while until he opened his heart with love and moved through it. Jesus was instantly standing in front of my friend at the moment he pushed through his heart with love. Jesus took him through the door that goes into the Initiation Room.

Jesus then initiated my friend into Level Four. I was invited to witness his Initiation. During his initiation I watched the pictures or movies shown about the past and the things to come in the oval on the floor. I felt honored to be allowed to see his initiation, since I'm not a Level Four.

CHAPTER FOURTEEN

Volunteering in the Level Three Room

Once, when I traveled to the White Light Room to do my volunteer work, I was surprised to see an extremely tall spirit at the back upper level of the room. This immense spirit nodded to me to go ahead and do my work. After helping a few deceased spirits, this powerful spirit motioned for me to go up to Him. I did.

The spirit explained "We've been watching you work" and it's been met with great approval. I was quite shocked about everything. I didn't know who I was talking to, so I had to ask. It turns out that this spirit, and the spirit behind him, came from a much higher Level.

Zeus was the one talking to me, and Apollo was standing behind him. I thought that Zeus, Apollo, and the stories about them were simply myths. What do I know!

The next time when I arrived in light body form to the large White Light Room to do volunteer work, there was another spirit there from a higher Level. I spoke to this spirit for a while. She explained that my project would now be under the supervision of Kate. I no longer needed to get permission before entering this room to work.

The next time I went to do my volunteer work, there was another spirit from a higher-Level waiting in the room for me. Her name is Aphrodite. She has been put in charge of this project. She explained that instead of me helping Levels One, Two, and Three, in the future each Level would have its own large room. I'm now working the Level Three room. I've since recruited volunteers to work the White Light Rooms Level One and Level Two.

I had no idea that doing this volunteer work would receive such attention. It all goes back to the Golden Rule: do unto others as you would have them do unto you.

I'm trying so hard to do the right thing. I wish that I always knew exactly what that is. Remember there is always someone behind you and someone ahead of you. This will help. When I see arrogant people, who seem to think that they're better or smarter than others, I realize that they just don't get what it's all about.

Later, a tall female visited the White Light Room when I was there. What a shocker. She's from the middle of the Milky Way, and the most advanced group that is now an extremely high Level; God's current Level. Kate is also from that Level.

I had no idea that there was such an advanced group, or that Kate was from it. If you compare them to us, they're like a huge computer system that can do more and run faster.

It turns out that there is a total of thirty-two different groups at different levels, between Level One and the highest Level that exists in the middle of the Milky Way. Groups advance, as they are ready.

Universal Worship

As more friends, relatives, and others who I knew died, I asked and received permission to help them. Pope John Paul II was one of those I was given permission to help. I was waiting for him at the time of his death. After he died, he told me to wait for a while. He spent forty-five minutes in the Vatican before joining me.

I escorted him to the small White Light Room (This was before the creation of the large White Light Rooms). We went through the same process as before, except when Jesus appeared to take him, he asked Jesus to wait for a minute. I'd previously never seen anyone ask Jesus to wait. Pope John Paul II wanted to talk to me first, before being initiated to Level Four. What on Earth could be so important as to ask Jesus to wait?

Pope John Paul II turned to me and told me that I've been waiting for him to die so he can help me finish my book. I didn't realize that John, the very tall spirit who'd visited me in the past in light body form, was the very same spirit as Pope John Paul II. He must have visited me during his sleeping hours. Then, Pope John Paul II turned to Jesus, and Jesus took him into the Initiation Room. Pope John Paul II was given a standing ovation by all the Initiates in the Assembly of the First Born. It was a beautiful Initiation. I was invited to watch. I used to hide behind my Guide by the doorway from the White Light Room during the Initiations.

I never feel as though I should be there to witness the Initiations, even though I'm invited to do so. Now, I've been given permission to sit straight out from the podium where Jesus does the initiations, and right behind the oval in the floor where the movies of the past and future, scenes that have come from the Lifeline room, are shown.

I finally figured out the reason I'm invited to watch. It's so I understand exactly what's going on so I can tell you all about it. I feel honored to get to sit there.

John Paul II is continuing to help me with this book. His goal while he was Pope was that he wanted to unite all the religions and all the churches before he died. He couldn't accomplish this. So now he's here with me helping me to write this book, in hopes that the information here will help all to understand that we're all here doing the same thing and trying to get to the same place.

We're all spiritually evolving under the same laws and the same God. He is here to oversee our development; to enforce the system of rules on Earth so that eventually we learn whether we want to or not. He is overseeing everything.

Now it's time to realize that we're all trying to get to the same place. We're all here trying to become a greater amount of love to make it to the next Level, in our case, Level Four. We're doing it in the best way we know how and usually in the religion that fits our belief system and in our own ways that we're familiar with. It doesn't matter which religion we choose to practice and learn how to be a loving person; although it is beneficial to be baptized. The important thing is that we learn to love unconditionally and make it to the next Level.

CHAPTER FIFTEEN

The Other Side: A Grand Tour

When I tell people, I've had a near-death experience, they want to know what it's like on the Other Side. So, did I. One day while I was cleaning house, Jesus came to me and said, "Come with me now."

Happy to have a break, I got comfy on the leather sofa in the living room and my light bodies left with Jesus for a tour of the Other Side. It was unbelievably fabulous. There's so much more going on there than I'd ever imagined.

I've seen the Other Side while traveling in my light bodies. Sometimes you may have funny dreams, where

151

you're doing one thing and then doing another thing. Normally you send out light bodies in teams of three. Three light bodies might go to check this out, and three others might have another mission. When your light bodies return, they bring back information and share it with the rest of your light bodies, hence; you experience dreams. You may also hear sounds or tones when your light bodies return. What happens is that when the returning light bodies share the information that they have gathered while they were out, you hear them giving the information to the rest of your light bodies and this sounds to you like tones or ringing in the ears.

Humans attend classes during sleep time. You study during the night and experience during waking hours. You have twelve light bodies within your physical form that travel during the time your physical body sleeps.

•••••

First Jesus took me to meet the Fairness Master. The Fairness Master is in control on all accounts of fairness. He is tall, thin, with dark hair and a long face shape. He has an eye like an eagle. Nothing gets past him unnoticed. The scales of justice that the ancient Egyptians painted are symbolic of the Fairness Master. The question is: "How fair have you been?"

He has the assignment of making sure that all things are fair; making sure no one is cheated or cheats others. If they do, there is retribution to pay. The Fairness

Master is always watching, and when things get out of line, the Fairness Master equalizes them. Believe me; he does a perfect job making sure everything in life winds up fair, either in this lifetime or in a future life-time.

That's why it's so important to be fair in everything in your life. If we're generous, then generosity comes our way. Something you want or need will come your way, and in a multiple of what you gave. It works at home, and it works at business. If you give a fair price, you receive a fair price. Taking advantage of other people sooner or later catches up to you. Something happens to even things out. Yes, we're back to what goes around comes around. Sometimes things might happen that aren't what goes around comes around, but there is a reason, ask "Why" and it can be a very interesting answer.

There are rooms to tally good deeds and many more rooms to tally up bad deeds. The bad tallies consist of black energy. There are many, many rooms of black energy room tallies and the number is growing. The good tallies, consisting of White Light, go to the room above the Fairness Master. When enough good tallies are counted, good things go back to the creator of them, and at the very best time imaginable!

Negative tallies vary in size from very small to im-mensely large. For example, if someone does something that does not comply with God's Laws, the information including their name and what they did goes into the appropriate room for the degree of wrongness. If it is a small thing, such as keeping five cents change instead of telling the cashier too much was given and returning the five cents, the offense goes into a small room. If the offense is large, such as murder, it goes into the appropriate larger room. Satan has a huge room filled with negative deeds.

Each of the tally rooms has Level Four workers. They work with both the Fairness Master and the Guardian Angels of those who have black marks in these tally rooms. At the very worst time for the person who earned the black mark, something bad will be returned to that person. If it is a small offense, it will be a small problem, if it is a huge offense, it will be intensified ten times and will be dispersed to that person at the worst time possible.

If we're stingy or greedy – watch out! Greed or worrying about anything that you have to be greedy about, can cause cancer! Cheat someone, and you'll be debited to a multiple of what you gained. This could be your water pipes breaking during a freeze, or maybe you'll rip your favorite piece of clothing, and you'll need to replace it. You never get away with cheating another. You'll pay sooner or later!

This isn't the same thing as negative thinking. With negative thinking, you put out what you don't want....

and the Universe works to give you exactly that. Take out the word don't, which the Universe does not register, and that's what you get, what you don't want.

Don't confuse that with the work of the Fairness Master. The Fairness Master isn't just concerned about money and goods. Time spending time, giving time, helping people learn and advance has huge spiritual value. Volunteer work always will bring something good back to you. That's cause and effect; you do something good for another and surprise, surprise, something good is done for you or comes to you usually at the best time possible.

Politicians talk about "taxes being fair." Their idea of "fair" is to take more from people who earn money and "give" it to those less fortunate. The way they say it makes it sound like they are the ones being fair and generous. They're really neither. It's not their money to give: the money belongs to the people who earn it. It's not really fair to either the person who gets it (because they will have to pay retribution) or the person it's taken away from.

Being "generous" with someone else's money isn't generosity. It's just a different form of being greedy: seeking to get and keep something that isn't yours or taking what isn't yours and giving it to another. This is so wrong! In this case, it's seeking power and popularity. This is not following the rules of the Fairness Master.

Beware.

Next, I was shown a wide and tall hallway.

On each side of the hall are doors that go into rooms of learning, or classrooms; in fact, there are ninety-three rooms now. There's a room for every subject that you can imagine. We have access to these rooms and knowledge. Most of us tend to go to them during the night while we're sleeping, but sometimes we take naps and go there while we are sleeping.

There's knowledge available on subjects such as accounting, economics, engineering, architecture, and art. There are rooms for learning about designing, drawing, government, languages, music, oil painting, psychology, and quilting. I saw rooms for learning science, sculpting, sewing, sociology, and sports of every kind, to name a few. There are rooms for learning to have more compassion, more humility, and more patience. There are rooms to go into to learn to be fair, generous, or kind. ANYTHING and everything you want to learn is available.

There is a hall like this for Level One; for humans at the beginning Level. There is one for Level Two; for those who have achieved an intermediate Level. And there is also a hall with Level Three rooms for learning. The Ones and Twos don't exactly get fairness very well. Threes do a good job of understanding fairness, because they understand that the most important thing about being a human being is to spiritually advance.

This is done by people becoming self-reliant. We are to evolve into decent, responsible, honorable, trustworthy, and truthful human beings. Giving someone a free ride does'nt promote spiritual growth. It stagnates or even reverses spiritual growth or the prson might even regress. Our purpose of life on this planet is to get to the next Level, and to do it in the quickest way possible. The faster we learn, the sooner we move on to the next Level.

Next, there was a dark circular room. This room is a combination of an amphitheater and a dark pit. The seats descend lower and lower into a darker and darker pit. This is where people congregate who are unfair and are usually greedy. The more unfair and the greedier the person, the lower they sit in the pit. I call this room the Greedy Pit.

Many will not be allowed to re-incarnate any more after they die. Many are lower than Level One. When they die, they'll be sent back to the species, or animal life, to the Level of love and consciousness they've become or have dwindled to.

There are some who are greedy and manipulate others. They earn lower and lower seats in this Money Pit. They are regressing or spiritually fading away, literally, to being less and less love. The worst of these are Satan's followers, and their time is expiring. Now as they die off, they're being sent to the Level of love that they have attained. In most cases, they are being sent back to the animal species, or, they may be turned to dust. When this happens, their souls cease to exist.

Next was the White Light Cloud Room. This is a room for extremely fair and generous people. Their feet never touch the floor; they seem to float lightly in the air. These are loving people: heart centered, generous, compassionate, kind, humble, and care immensely about others. They have become wealthy by following Gods' laws. God intends for us to follow his laws. Do that and we can have it all. God has promised that if we obey His commandments, that everything that is His is ours. We're to learn the lesson of generosity and make donations for good causes; this does not include the: you scratch my back and I'll scratch yours, scenarios. More money will be generously given as donations if people aren't paying such high taxes.

Atlantis fell due to a lack of love and an overdevelopment of consciousness or intelligence. Love must always exceed intelligence on this planet to continue to spiritually evolve to a higher Level. Those who have earned the right to go into the White Cloud Room have followed God's laws. This is true success. These are highly evolved Level Threes who get to enter this room. No one in this room would ever be arrogant. The arrogant ones are most often found in the Money Pit.

Only a few people were in the White Cloud room the first time it. was shown to me. Now there are more there, as people are learning to become more heart centered, or are learning to think with their hearts or heart brain, to be more specific, and are becoming more generous and thoughtful of others. Yes, your heart actually has a brain. The brain uses compassion and wants to help others advance. This means that each person needs to work to spiritually advance. Someone else cannot do this for another.

Each and every person must learn the necessary lessons on their own. They learn through experience and by observing others; what works and what doesn't work. Most likely, whatever the lesson is, we've all been there and done that in some lifetime or another or will be there and do that. Now, that could be a scary thought!

Eventually, if we're lucky and work diligently, we'll make it to this room. The next place to go to after this room is Level Four when we become perfect love. This is the next Level for Threes, and we're always trying to make it to the next higher Level.

Then there is the Tapestry Room. It's also known as the Lifeline Room, the Akashic Records room, the Hall of Records, or the Book of Life.

Each individual line contains a complete history from the moment God created the speck of energy that went into the amoeba to start growing into consciousness and love. Every thought we think, every word we speak, and every deed we do is stored on our individual lifelines. The future has alternative lines, with paths waiting to be chosen. We have choices to make. God gives us free will as to when we want to learn and which path we choose to take. We can learn now, or we can learn later.

The Guardian of the Tapestry Room guards this room. If you desire to be admitted to this room, you must first get permission from this room's Guardian. He's really tall and buff, like a bouncer. You approach the Guardian of the room with the guidance of your personal Guide, and you use formal language.

You say "Please" when you ask for permission to enter, and you say "thank you" when you leave. This is very important, because on this Level everything is done in formal language with great respect for all. If you forget to do this, entrance will be denied you. If you forget to be thankful when you leave, you may not be admitted the next time you request it.

After being admitted to this room, ask your Guide to help you to imprint the skills or knowledge you desire. If you go alone, and this is only for more advanced students, you look around for the energy structure or pattern that you wish to attain. You then approach this energy, which is contained on a lifeline; you ask the energy to give you a copy of the information stored within the energy pattern. A copy will be made and stored in your energy field, like making a copy on your computer. You now have an energy imprint or copy of the desired information. This is what I call, "Imprinting."

Imprinting can be used for many things, such as imprinting a skill in a preferred sport such as golf, polo, tennis, soccer, water polo, swimming, diving, basketball, baseball, football, or even coaching skills. It can help in organizational skills, business skills, sales skills, architecture, engineering, cooking, sewing, speaking, or pretty much any skill you can think of. Imprinting the desired ability or skill will give you the patterns you've requested. You'll have acquired the "natural ability" that some others may have been born with. It may take time to integrate this information. Now it'll be available for you to use anytime you choose. Imprinting can give you the natural abilities that you've always wished for. Be careful not to over imprint or you may feel full, similar to your computer being out of space. As in anything you do, ask for guidance.

These lines are available to others for imprinting or general information that may be needed by another.

Many times, this room has been used for imprinting patterns before we are born. A Guide will help us to look for the perfect knowledge needed for the future lifetime. Upon being born, we arrive with certain skills and knowledge stored in our own fields or subconscious. We are endowed with abilities that are going to be helpful for us to use in this lifetime. If we haven't attained these abilities through our own experience, then we're taken to this room and with the help of our Guides, we're imprinted with additional energy patterns that have been attained by others. Look at young children today. They pick up a remote control or a cell phone and seem to know how to use them. In general, my generation was not born with that natural ability.

Think that your lifeline is private? It is not.

Upon entering the room, you can ask for certain information to light up, so that you can find what you're looking for and access the needed information. You may not misuse this room or the information in it. If you do misuse the information in this room, you will no longer be admitted into it. There are always consequences for your behavior. Cause and effect. Good or bad. Preferable or undesirable. You shall reap what you have sown.

There's a room called Heaven's Helpers. God directs prayers to this room. In this room are helpers to respond to prayers, whether the prayers are for physical or mental problems. On the white door to this room is written Heaven's Helpers. The door has four rectangular windows in the top third of the door. This room always has at least a couple of Holy Spirits or Guides in it. If there are many spirits in the room at the time the prayer is sent, then anyone of them will respond to the prayer, or they will call a Spirit who specializes in the "problem" involved in the prayer. In any event, someone is immediately sent to help answer the prayer. Hence, the title of the room is self-explanatory, for these are truly "Heaven's Helpers."

Once I was blessed with the opportunity to witness what happens to prayer energy. I was with a small group of people walking around the neighborhood. One of my walking partners remarked that her back hurt. I offered to work on her back and clear off the black toxic negative energy, but my offer was declined. Another person in the group immediately stopped walking and said a prayer to God for the other person's sore back to be healed.

I decided to follow in light body form, the energy created from the prayer. It went up into the heavens and a large hand came out from above and redirected the prayer energy to the Heaven's Helper Room. I believe that the hand that I saw came from the person on duty for answering prayers. A Holy Spirit who is one of Heaven's Helpers was dispensed and instantly was standing behind the person with the sore back. This healer was wearing a white robe and had golden light eyes. The Spirit sent from this room started to release the stress from her spinal cord. He removed black toxic energy from her physical form, concentrating on the spine.

I stood there in excitement because I've been taught how to do this. I silently spoke to the Holy Spirit who was doing the healing work and commented to him that I've been taught how to do this work. He answered, "Shhh.... They aren't ready for this information yet."

I stood there blessed with the knowledge of understanding how some of the things work on the Other Side. I was also disappointed that the person had declined my help since I've been trained to do this work. Kate has given me extensive lessons in energy healing. There are expert healers available in the healing room, which may be called to help, if there isn't a healer available in the Heaven's Helper room. You can also go to the healing room to train to be a healer. People who have Healing Hands have been trained there. Even doctors go there to learn more about how to help their patients. So "Heaven's Helpers" are in the healing room, and Heaven's Helpers are in the room that answers prayers.

Next, down the hall, I was shown the Invention Room. It was amazing. I walked past invention after invention. Anything and everything that has ever been invented or ever will be invented is in this room. The room is massive; the different inventions go on and on. I just stood there marveling at how massive the room is; much larger than the other rooms that Jesus has shown me so far. As with all the rooms, the walls and ceilings are made up of White Light.

Anyone from our planet who is a Level One, Two, or Three can go in to get new ideas for new inventions. This is so impressive. There are things that we haven't even dreamed of yet. This room can activate the imagination for one who visits it during sleep hours. You might start imagining new and different things after waking up. When you wake up, try to remember what you saw there. New inventions from this room are just on the brink of being remembered, and then can be manifested on this Level.

I've been shown a Viewing Room of the past and the future on Level Four. This is where visions come from. It's like a small movie theatre. You ask to see something, and voila, it is shown to you.

CHAPTER SIXTEEN

Ghost Stories

The first time I ever saw someone from the Other Side happened at a slumber party when I was fourteen. Since then, I've had plenty of contact with the Other Side. I've also seen plenty of ghosts, particularly in the last few years. That's because my husband and I travel a lot and stay in old hotels all over the world. Ghosts like to hang around old buildings for a good reason.

Usually, the reason a ghost didn't cross over to the Other Side is because something traumatic happened at the time of their death. So, they chose to stay where that happened, and not cross over. Today there are no new ghosts because when someone dies, they are no longer allowed to stay as a ghost.

That's not what most people understand. One time I watched a TV show about ghosts that really upset me. Showing no compassion for the spirit, the expert would ask "Hello. Is there an entity present?" That's when I prayed and asked if I could help ghosts cross over. A larger White Light Room was created for bringing ghosts across. Since then, helping ghosts has been a pet project of mine.

By now, many ghosts from many different places have now crossed over. For example, most of the Holocaust victims and many of the Egyptian Pharaoh's servants who were buried alive have crossed over. Still, there are a few here and there who didn't choose to cross over.

On Dec. 21, 2012, Jesus commanded all the ghosts to cross over. There is a White Light room that is five football fields long that had been prepared for them for the process.

I used to run into a lot of ghosts. Many of them just wanted to be left alone. Others wanted to be noticed, wanted help, and were quite social. Like the time one tapped me on my shoulder. I was at art class, eating lunch with one of my fellow art students, Danna. We were at a tearoom in an old building in Georgetown,

Texas.

I had already helped several ghosts from downtown Georgetown cross over to the Other Side. There was one ghost who had chosen not to cross over. Ghosts still have free will, and it's not up to me to force them to cross over. I simply offered to help them if they wish to be helped.

So, at lunch on this particular day, the ghost who had chosen not to cross over came up behind me while my friend, Danna and I were eating lunch. He started tapping me on my back on my right shoulder. Tap, tap, tap. Again, tap, tap, tap. Then, a harder tap, tap, tap.

Danna was in the middle of telling me something, and I didn't want to interrupt her. I was waiting for her to finish before mentally answering the ghost.

The ghost was very anxious for me to pay attention. The ghost decided to go one step further and move my soda can that was sitting above my knife on the table surface. He moved it to the right, then to the left, and then he moved it up towards my friend's plate, then back towards my plate.

Danna stopped talking and pointed at my soda can, stuttering to me that my soda can was moving around. She immediately picked it up and explained to me that there was no condensation on the can. Next she checked to see if the table was wobbling, and no, it wasn't.

She asked me if I noticed my soda moving back and forth. I answered her "Yes." There is a ghost tapping me on my shoulder, and I didn't respond fast enough, so he started moving my soda can, to get my attention."

I then found out from the ghost that he had changed his mind and that he would in fact, like help moving to the Other Side. I asked Danna if she could wait for just a minute or two, while I helped this ghost. Mission accomplished, said ghost moved to the Other Side, and my friend and I finished both our conversation and our lunch.

This isn't unusual for me for a ghost to tap me on the shoulder, but they normally don't move my soda can back and forth.

California

My husband and I have traveled to Benicia many times over the past several years. We usually stay at a bed and breakfast that's over a hundred years old, if it's available. It has quite a history. It has been transformed from a brothel. It turns out that the hotel is haunted. I know this because I found out firsthand.

We have a favorite room that we like to stay in. One time when we got there, our reserved room had accidentally been given to someone else. Travesty! The desk clerk sent us to the Red Room on the third floor. Instantly, I didn't want to go to that room.

When we entered the room, I was picking up strange energy, which made me feel uneasy, to say the least. As my husband poured a bath and got into it, I took off my shoes and sat up on an antique bed that had probably been there for a very, very long time. I didn't like the feeling in the room, I didn't like the heavy brocade bedspread, or the red wallpaper. I felt very uneasy.

I was very tired from traveling, so I closed my eyes to rest. I wasn't in ghost mode. In other words, I didn't have my mind in the right place to help move ghosts across to the Other Side. Usually, when I go out to find ghosts and help them to move to the Other Side, I find them and help them without ever experiencing their emotions. That's not the case with what happened next.

I was sitting on the bed relaxing when suddenly I started seeing different ghosts. I not only saw what happened to them, I felt their emotions at the time of their deaths. This was overwhelming. I was completely freaked out!

First, I saw a girl in her early twenties. She appeared to me, what I saw at first was her head, with her throat having been slit; I was horrified. Then I saw what had happened. One of her customers had fallen in love with her. He was married, so he couldn't take her away and marry her. He was terribly jealous and couldn't stand the fact that she worked as a lady of the night. He couldn't stand it that she would let other men touch her. He loved her more than life itself.

After making love to her that night, he followed her out of bed and slit her throat. He spoke words of love to her as she was watching the knife move across her throat in the reflective surface. She couldn't believe that the one and only person she trusted was doing this to her. Her body went limp, slid down his and hit the floor.

He sobbed uncontrollably; he had just killed the woman he loved with all his heart. He was distraught. His dark brown hair drooped, and his long thin face grimaced with sorrow and pain. He took the blood-drenched knife and plunged it into his own heart. His body then fell down partially on top of hers, and partially beside hers. The floor was covered with their blood.

I wasn't in ghost working mode and wasn't prepared to see this. I both saw what happened to them and felt their emotions! Obviously, they had not moved on across to the Other Side. They needed help.

Then, I saw a young girl who was fourteen. She had run

away from home and ended up in the brothel. She had her first sexual experience there. In that room. Afterwards, crying hysterically, she slit both of her wrists. She dropped to the floor and sobbed furiously until she passed out and died. She couldn't believe that she had become a whore, and couldn't live with herself, so she took her own life. Her emotions were off the wall. The feelings that I felt from her were extreme.

After that, I saw a man who had been hung. He was black and was innocent of the crime he had been accused of, but that didn't matter. He had been accused of the deaths of the first two, the slit throat, and the stabbing. He was the scapegoat for their deaths. He was a kindly man. He had frantic emotions at the time of his death.

After seeing these ghosts, I jumped off the tall bed, went into the bathroom and announced to my husband that we needed to go to another hotel immediately. I didn't tell him why.

When I called the front desk, the owner's son convinced us to move rooms, and not leave the hotel. We did move to another room that was on the second floor, just below our favorite room. The next morning, I went back to the Red Room and helped the ghosts move across to the Other Side. I was in my mode to help ghosts and not experience their emotions.

Later that day, after picking my husband up at work, we returned to the hotel. We went up to our room. I locked the door with the deadbolt lock. My husband went over to the TV to get the remote control and turn it on. I got comfortable sitting on the bed.

All of a sudden, the bedroom door flew open, and a very tall ghost rushed in. He demanded to know where I had taken his friends. Oh, he was furious! I don't know about you, but I was extremely uncomfortable having a ghost mad at me and wasn't quite sure how this was going to turn out! He had just blown open a dead bolted door.

I was doing a bit of the Texas Two Step as I explained to him that I had taken them across to the Other Side, and that I would be happy to take him if he wanted, and that he didn't have to stay if he didn't want to. He agreed. I took him across, and he decided to return and not stay. Later, after two trips back to this bed and breakfast, I was finally able to help him cross to the Other Side.

All the ghosts in this small, beautiful town have now moved across to the Other Side. Thank you, God!

Seattle

It was the middle of the night in Seattle. My husband was out of town, and I was alone in our condo. Suddenly, I awoke with someone's hands wrapped around my neck. I was being strangled. What was going on?

I looked over to my right and saw three of my light bodies. They returned from working while I was sleeping. They look terrible, as though they have been beaten up.

Now I get it: this ghost who had his hands on my neck had followed my light bodies back to my physical form. This male ghost was trying to kill me. He was so angry. It took all my strength to push this ghost away from me. I felt fear; I was struggling and trying to get this ghost off of me. Quick thinking and SUCCESS!

OK, he's off of me.

The first thing out of my mouth was, "What's your problem? Why are you trying to kill me?" The ghost explained: "You've taken all my friends away", in an exasperating tone.

"OK." I answered, "What do you want to do about it? Have you changed your mind, and do you want to move across to the Other Side with them?"

The ghost told me he was lonely without his friends around. I asked him if I could take him where I had taken the others. I told him If he didn't want to stay on the Other Side, he could return. It's amazing what a little kindness will do: he agreed to investigate what happened to his friends on the Other Side.

I took him to the Dining Room on the Other Side. Within minutes, Angels had brought some of his friends who had chosen to cross over. The ghost then chose to stay with his friends. He was taken to the appropriate White Light Room. He had accumulated enough love to be a Level Two. He was processed in the Level Two White Light Room and was now back into the system in order to continue spiritually evolving. This ghost is now where he's supposed to be; crossed over and continuing to learn.

I was surprised my Guides allowed this ghost to try to strangle me. I asked why they didn't stop him. They told me they could see the outcome and knew that I could take care of myself and would be able to push the ghost away from me. But they didn't tell me the rest of the story of what else they could see happening in the future. More of this story later.

There is another Seattle ghost story that happened involving Chief Seattle. He is a short little guy with an almost square face. The Chief was definitely in charge of the seventy-seven ghosts there.

My friend and I had finished another set of exercises on the stairs and headed out for a walk. It was a beautiful day. We found ourselves down at the Alki Point Lighthouse. We took the tour and afterwards went outside to enjoy the view. My friend asked me if there were any ghosts. I said that I hadn't shifted my frequency to take a look. I shifted and looked for ghosts and to my surprise, standing right beside me was Chief Seattle. He hadn't tapped my shoulder, so I had not noticed him.

I asked him if he wanted to move across now. I explained that when Dec. 21, 2012, came along, that he and his friends would have to go across and it would be easier for them to move now when they could get more attention. He left and spoke with the group.

He came back over to me, and the answer was yes, they wanted to go. It all went very well except for this one little troublemaker. What to do about him?

The rest of the group made it to Level Four, but he didn't deserve to be a Four. I had to ask Jesus what to do. I wanted him to go with his group because they would keep track of him. If I had been the little one, I would not have wanted to be the only one going somewhere else.

I guess there is an exception for every rule. Jesus allowed this little guy to go with his group, but on probation. They are doing a very good job of helping this little guy spiritually develop. I later checked on his progress: he has now opened his heart and mind to God. You're not supposed to get to go to Level Four unless your heart and mind are already open to God. Thank you Jesus for your wisdom and compassion!

Chief Seattle and his entire group have now crossed over!

Rothenberg, Germany

Two weeks later, after the choking incident, we flew to Germany. When my husband had a break, we spent a week playing tourist. First, we headed towards Bavaria, and stopped in a famous old town, Rothenberg.

Rothenberg had cobblestone streets and a town square with a town clock. When the clock chimed on the hour, two mechanical people, one on each side of the clock, appeared when the windows opened. There was a moving female on the right side of the clock, and a male on the left side, raising his beer up to seemingly take a drink, and down again. Then the windows would close.

We had reservations at a hotel that used to be the home of a very wealthy man. We stayed in the room that used to be the Throne Room. Peasants would come with chickens or food to pay their taxes or ask for favors.

It was winter, and the tile floor was very cold. The room had windows that were very old with bubbles in the glass of the windowpanes. There was an arch between the sitting room and the bedroom, and the ceiling was quite low. We had to be careful not to hit our heads. The bathroom was large. The window curtains were made of heavy old-fashioned fabric that seemed to be ancient and gave the room the feeling of having gone back in time.

While we were there, I busied myself with trying to help ghosts move across to the Other Side. If ghosts choose not to go, it's their choice. I was able to help several ghosts move across. One ghost, who had chosen not to cross over, changed his mind. He came to our bedside during the time I was out of body helping the other ghosts. This ghost, not being able to find me, tapped my husband on the shoulder. It was a very firm tap. He wanted my husband to take him across.

Now, in the first place, my husband was skeptical about all ghosts. Up until this time, the only thing he had noticed was the bedroom door flying open in Benicia, CA. He really wasn't too sure about any ghost business at all. In other words, he was the wrong person to tap. My husband woke up when the ghost tapped his shoulder. He looked over at me, and I was sound asleep on the other side of the bed. He looked around the room, and NO ONE was there. Yet, someone just had tapped his shoulder. Shocker! When I returned from out of body work, I helped this ghost join the others.

Guess what, he now believes in ghosts!

Kronberg

Later during the trip, we checked into the Schloss Hotel

in Kronberg, Germany. This was a very deluxe hotel that was once a castle. We stayed in a beautiful room in one of the towers. It was circular, with the prettiest wallpaper with pink roses, green leaves, and a white background. The furniture was antique like the kind that is roped off at Hearst Castle in California. There was a love seat with two Queen Anne chairs and a coffee table, a desk with a chair, an armoire, bed, two nightstands, a beautiful bachelor's chest, and a beautiful Persian carpet. There was a beautiful crystal chandelier hanging from the domed ceiling.

My husband was tired from teaching all day. So, he started a bath and got into the tub. I finished unpacking and then found one of the Queen Anne chairs. The moment I sat down, I heard a sweet, kindly voice tell me, "This is my room."

It was a ghost. She was a petit little woman, wearing a dark green long elegant dress with a light-colored lace collar and cuffs. The dress had pleats at the waistline and there was some lace ruffled on the front. The fabric seemed to be like a brocade cotton print. It was a lovely expensive dress. The ghost told me again, "This is my room."

I told her I loved the room. Did she mind if we stayed in her room? She said that she liked us and that she was happy to have us stay in the room. I thought that was good news: we don't need to try to change rooms. I've had to do that a time or two when we stayed in other old hotels. Most of them used to have a ghost or two hanging around.

I wondered who she was. Her dress suggested she was very well off, but the building had been around for more than a century. Built by the daughter of Queen of England, and widow of a German Emperor.

The ghost answered, "Victoria Em . . . . Em . . . Fred."

I couldn't quite understand what her middle or last name was. It didn't sound like any female name that I'm familiar with. But this was Germany. "Em" or something? The last name sounded like Fred.

I did what I normally did in situations like this. I asked her, "Would you like to go to a nice dining room to have a lovely dinner?"

She said that she would love to go with me. I took her across to the Other Side to Kate's dining room. When we got there, many of her loved ones were there to greet her. She knew so many people, and she was well loved. She had such a sweet personality and a gentle way about her, I can see why.

This ghost, Victoria, chose to cross over to the Other Side. She was taken to White Light Room Level Three. As you know, White Light Room Level Three is the room that I volunteer in. I went into the White Light Room and gave her instructions on what she was supposed to do while in that room and asked if she would like help.

Of course, she said, "Yes." In a short period of time, she moved through her heart with love, and Jesus appeared instantly and took her into the Initiation Room. Jesus Initiated her into Level Four; remember, "You can't get there but by me", Jesus said. Then Jesus Initiated her into Level Four.

Success! Victoria is no longer a ghost and is exactly where she's supposed to be.

All that happened in the time it took my husband to take his bath. He does love his soaking baths. After he got out of the tub, he went to the desk to work on his computer. I told him the story about the sweet lady ghost. He listened patiently. (I'm blessed with the most wonderful husband!).

A few minutes later my husband found a pamphlet and exclaimed, "Listen to this." He read the story of the hotel we were staying in. "This is the Victoria Empress Fredrick "schloss" castle."

Victoria was England's Queen Victoria's oldest daughter; she married the German Prince Fredrick and built this castle after he died. He died 99 days after becoming Kaiser.

Wow! I didn't know that I had just helped an Empress.

I help whoever needs to be helped. There is no requirement, other than they are a person who needs to be helped.

The very next day, I'm called in light body form, and two spirits have a gift for me. It is a Golden Light Crown. I don't know if it is OK for me to accept such a gift. I'm not quite sure who's trying to give it to me. I ask Jesus if it's OK for me to receive the crown. He didn't answer. I had to figure this one out on my own.

I thought at first maybe it was being given by friends of Victoria Empress Fredrick. I felt like I couldn't accept such a reward for simply volunteering. After all, that was my volunteer assignment from the Other Side. If I'm doing a sort of volunteer assignment, I shouldn't be given such a beautiful reward just because Victoria had a status.

The two spirits who were trying to award me with this golden light crown told me to look around. I didn't realize we were in an assembly room. Oh, my goodness! The room was filled with high Level spirits, and the two standing beside me are the top two spirits from a much higher Level. Their energy is so refined that it's hard for me to see them. I see them as energy. Remember, I'm only a lowly Level Three peon in comparison. Boy, did I feel inferior.

The Grand Spirits explained to me that the Golden

Crown is being awarded to me for helping the ghost who tried to kill me by strangulation. They said my immediate response of "Get off of me" and "Why are you trying to kill me?" and "How can I help you?" was exactly what "Love thy neighbor" is all about. They explained that there are only four Level Threes, including me, who've been awarded this Golden Energy Crown.

I don't feel as though I deserve anything special for helping this ghost. If I were a ghost, I would appreciate being helped. I know how to help the ghosts cross over: isn't that simply the right thing to do? Aren't we supposed to use our God-given talents for the good of everyone even angry ghosts?

Helping is such a simple thing to do. Just stop the ghost from trying to kill me, find out what the problem is, and solve the problem. Zeus and Apollo were the two higher Level spirits who were awarding me this light energy crown, or halo as we might call it. The theater was filled with higher Level spirits who gave me a standing ovation. I'm just a peon compared to all of them. I felt so underserving.

• • • •

Maybe there is more to helping others than I realized.

Loving thy neighbor is helping the other person or ghost, as the case may be. It is caring about the other person. It's being kind to the other person. Loving might be too strong of a word to use. Caring about others and being kind, patient, and generous, is where it's at. I had no idea that helping the angry ghost was such a big deal.

The moral of the story is simple: be kind to others and try to help them when you can.

CHAPTER SEVENTEEN

Rainbow Meditation

You never quite know what kind of curve balls the Universe will throw you. I had always wanted to go back and get a master's degree. At one point I went back to school and took all the required courses in psychology, thinking that maybe I'd get a degree in counseling. But with so much going on with two small kids, there really wasn't time for that. Instead, I was the Soccer Mom.

A friend of mine had converted an extra bedroom into a library, and I went over to help her move her books out of the boxes. She had a lot of books to put up on the new shelves. That was because she was working on a Master of Science degree in a program called Studies

185

of the Future. While we were unpacking, she told me all about the program: that it teaches how to be a consultant and how to help CEO's or companies plan their future. It's an extremely left brained program. Since we live near Johnson Space Center that meant that mainly NASA engineers were enrolled in this program. But there was one particular class in the program that teaches how to be more intuitive: Visionary Futures.

Now, that class was right up my alley.

As I was pulling the books out of the boxes, I got really excited about several of the books. My friend said I could borrow any of them I would like to read. Oh, I liked this book and that book, and my friend starts telling me that I ought to get in touch with one of her professors. I did, and he invited me to visit his class.

I arrived at the class at the designated time, introduced myself to her professor and sat down to visit the class. Then something happened that changed the next few years in my life: he introduced me as a new student who was joining the class. Hello, graduate school!

I'd been a test subject at NASA, a room Mom at the grade school, a Cub Scout leader for both boys, I taught teenage girls for the teen board at Sakowitz, and still modeled a little bit. Suddenly, I had become a graduate student. Something that I'd wanted to do for a long time. But I didn't think it would happen this way. This happened a few years before my near-death experience. So, now I'm a student.

One night as I fell asleep, I was completely absorbed trying to decide what on earth I was going to do for my project for my Visionary Futures class. I wanted to come up with a project that would help reduce stress, depression, and anxiety for people from grade school to old age. I wanted to give them a way to relax, sort things out, and come up with solutions to their problems. All so they could feel better because stress produces so many diseases.

I woke up in the middle of the night seeing a vision in color. This definitely was not a normal, black and white dream.

What I was shown was a rainbow of color. I was taken up through each of the colors of the rainbow, one color at a time. While in each color, I was told to let go of every negative thought, feeling, and emotion. First, I did this with the red color; then the orange color; then yellow and on through all the colors of the rainbow.

When I reached the top of the rainbow, purple, I was taken into the white color. This is a meditation room not to be confused with the White Light Rooms where people go when they die.

After reaching the White Light Meditation Room, all of the negative energy that has been released from my system was collected and called up to the violet color of the rainbow. This negative energy was purified by the violet light or by the amethyst light and was transformed back into positive energy or White Light.

How amazing!

So that vision became my class project. I called it Rainbow Meditation. I wrote it up for a class project, but it's a wonderful way to reduce stress, get rid of old hurts, and solve problems.

Here's the meditation.

Rainbow Meditation

Get into a comfortable position. If you're sitting, sit with your feet flat on the floor, and set your hands on your lap. As a way to help you to relax, you can take a deep breath and slowly let it out. Take another deep breath, and again, slowly let it out. Do this until you're completely relaxed. If you have a key word that you use in order to relax, you may use it now. If your eyes aren't already closed, you may close them now.

You may begin to feel more and more relaxed. You're going deeper and deeper and you may feel more and more relaxed. In fact, you may find yourself feeling extremely relaxed. As you are feeling more and more relaxed, focus for a moment on your heartbeat. Imagine that in the middle of your heart is a white flame. Concentrate on this flame and feel the love and harmony pulsating within it. You may begin to feel a connection to God.

Now, focus your attention on the middle of your forehead. This is the pituitary gland, and is also known as the third eye, or sixth chakra. As you're focusing on this gland, you may feel deeply relaxed, and may begin to feel light, in fact, very light. You may begin feeling so light that you may seem to float or rise upwards. There's a beautiful rainbow just above you, and on the other side of the rainbow is a room filled with white light that we'll enter after we rise up through the rainbow.

As you're feeling lighter and lighter, your light body many seem to float out and rise above your physical body. You may seem to feel so light that you float up into the red color. As you do that, if any of the colors of the rainbow change, it's ok, because your personal energy may mix with the energy of any rainbow color, and the color may vary. Absorb the Red energy into your light bodies and physical form. Feel the red energy move through your body. As it's absorbed, you can hear the sound of the red energy resonate with parts of your body. You're strengthened with it and you may feel the presence of power and vitality, a will to live, a physical power and feelings of being secure and well grounded. Let go of any negative thoughts, feelings and emotions.

As you move higher and higher, you may leave the negative thoughts, feelings, and emotions, in the red color, and move on into the orange level of the rainbow.

Let this orange energy penetrate through you. Fill yourself with a flow of joy. Orange is the color representing love, and symbolizes the system's energies, both physical and mental. Now you may let go of any negative

thoughts, feelings, and emotions, and leave them behind you in the orange energy as you move up into the
yellow energy of the rainbow.

Let the yellow energy flow through you. You may open
yourself up to new or improved ideas and patterns. Let
the yellow sunshine, the sweetness of life fill you. Look
at the bright sunshine of life. Now you may let go of
any negative thoughts, feelings, and emotions and
leave them behind you in the yellow energy. Fill yourself with the willingness to face new experiences and
feel a warm glow about you, as you move on up to the
green energy of the rainbow.

Let the green energy flow through you. Breathe in
openness to life. Let go of any negative thoughts, feelings, or emotions and leave them in the green energy
as you move on into the blue area of the rainbow.

The blue energy is now flowing through you. Feel your
ability to take in and assimilate. Be true to yourself.
This blue energy will help you develop your inner self
and gain enlightenment through personal development. You may now leave negative thoughts, feelings,
and emotions in the blue energy. Now move into the
indigo, blue-red color of the rainbow.

The indigo or blue-red energy is now flowing through
you. Feel a growing capacity to visualize and understand mental concepts and fill yourself with idealism
and imagination. Merge your inner vision with your
outer vision. You may now let go of any negative

thoughts, feelings, and emotions and leave them in the indigo energy.

Continue up into the violet area of the rainbow. Let this violet energy flow through you. Feel the soothing energy and the feeling of Oneness with God. Sense your divine purpose, and the total control of your thoughts, of attained wisdom and spirituality. You may feel knowing and intuition flowing through you. There's a sense of unlimited consciousness that goes beyond matter, energy, time, and space. Let the violet energy calm your mind; you may leave any negative thoughts, feelings, and emotions in the violet energy now and you may move up out of the rainbow into a meditation room filled with white light. You're now feeling serene and peaceful.

As you look back to the rainbow, watch as all of the negative thoughts, feelings, and emotions that you left behind, rise up one by one into the violet area of the rainbow to be purified or cleaned.

The violet energy is now changing all of the negative energy that you left behind and is transforming it into positive energy of bright white light. This energy is now being given back to you. You may receive it now and thank the rainbow for transforming the negative energy into positive energy. You may be feeling empowered from this transformation, for you are now vibrating at a higher rate or frequency. Feel how good this light vibration feels. Let positive thoughts freely move through your mind, and let insights come to you. You may feel extremely mellow and peaceful.

191

Now you may move on up the White Light Room. While you're in the White Light Room you can let thoughts and ideas come to you, or you may do one of the options given later.

There are choices at the end of this meditation to do while you're in the White Light Room. You may choose to do one of these now or to simply continue the meditation at this time.

Continue the Meditation

Now, we'll go back down through the rainbow. Move on into the violet energy now. Feel the soothing vibration and Oneness with the Creative Power. Move from the White light or the violet energy. Then move into the indigo energy and merge your inner vision with your outer vision and note your capacity to visualize and understand mental concepts.

Leaving the indigo energy and entering the blue energy, feel your personal development blossoming. Now, leaving the blue energy and entering the green energy, fill yourself with a deep sense of love and harmony. Going from the green energy to the yellow energy, breathe in the sweetness of life, feel great pleasure and expansiveness, feel spiritual wisdom and who you are within the universe.

Move from the yellow energy to the orange energy. Feel the unlimited love and harmony in your relationships. Notice how effectively you use your energies, both mental and physical. Move from the orange energy to the red energy and notice your ability to adequately display your emotions and feelings. Feel your positive thoughts and positive self-esteem.

Now leaving the rainbow, you may re-enter your physical body. You may be feeling relaxed, refreshed, and empowered. Notice the higher, lighter vibration your body is now pulsating at. This is due to negative thoughts, feeling, and emotions having been transformed into positive energy.

I'm now going to count from ten to one, and during this time, your awareness will return, and you will open your eyes when you're ready, feeling better than before, comfortable and aware of your surroundings. Ten, nine, eight......one.

End of Rainbow Meditation

The Rainbow meditation and method of relaxation, projection, and visualization can be used with not only adults, but also with children of all ages. Using a method such as this throughout the educational years and adulthood will provide an opportunity of getting in touch with your own intuition and of having less stress during your lifetime. Being able to relax and project into possible futures and being able to figure out the best possibility should help reduce anxiety and stress.

A well-known reaction to stress is to develop an addiction of one kind or another to use as a vice. It may be overeating, sex, smoking, drinking, drugs, or a variety of others. Stress is also linked to diseases such as cancer, leukemia, and lupus. Stress can also contribute to or cause heart attacks. Reduce stress, change negative thoughts to positive thoughts, eliminate negative thought patterns, and the end result is a healthier and happier you.

This meditation helps to clear negative and toxic energy out of your energy bodies, or aura as some people call it. This leads to better health, and you'll be able to think more clearly and feel more relaxed.

Options to do while in the White Light Meditation Room

The Tapestry Room

From the White Light Meditation Room, you can see an expansive, beautiful tapestry containing many strands in several different colors. Study this tapestry for a while. One strand has caught your attention. First, get permission from the Guardians of the tapestry, and approach the strand that you are attracted to. Look at this strand. It is comprised of several threads. These threads within the strand are each different possibilities in the future.

You may now enter the strand; choose a thread within it and travel along it. What do you see and feel? Do you like this possibility? After spending some time here, try another thread. What happens in this thread's future? If you have questions in your mind about the future, ask the questions now. Follow through different threads within your strand, one at a time, and see what the different future possibilities are.

Tapestry Room: College Option

If you are looking for what to major in, in college, go down one thread with one major in mind, and another thread with another major in mind, etc. Spend some time doing this now. See what you like to do, what courses you like to take and how well you do in them, and what you have a natural talent for and prefer doing.

Tapestry Room: Career Search Option

If you are trying to choose a career, go down one thread and look at the future for this career, and notice different available job choices in this career area by looking at different intersecting threads. Choose a job and see if you are enjoying it. Spend some time now going down different threads in order to check out different career and job possibilities. Do you like the hours of work? Do you like the pay? Do you work with people? Do you like the people you work with, if any? Do you like the way you dress for the job? Are you happy with this job? Explore different threads until you feel peaceful about the information you have gained from this exploration.

When you're finished seeing your future possibilities, you may return to the White Light Meditation Room. Review the different possibilities and store these thoughts into memory. Then finish going down through the Rainbow of colors to finish the meditation.

Be creative and think of another possibility. Use this meditation to become a healthier and happier person.

CHAPTER EIGHTEEN

The Genius of Jesus

One night before I fell asleep, I asked Jesus if He could please explain the mystery of Communion. I had meditated on this. "Do this in memory of me." What exactly does this mean? What was Jesus trying to tell us? What is this symbolic of?

It remained a mystery to me until one morning I awoke around 4:30 A.M. and Jesus explained it to me. So here we go.

To simplify this in the easiest way possible, Jesus explained that the body is symbolic of God's word, and the blood is symbolic of love. Love is the energy or frequency of God's love that flows through our bodies. In Communion we are being reminded to live God's word and to live with the energy of love continually flowing through us. Jesus's blood is pure unconditional love. Unconditional love forgives completely.

We are to speak God's words and become the embodiment of pure love. We are to become what Jesus is. When we become the embodiment of love, we will ascend in physical form to Level Four.

Jesus, with as many other great teachers of the past, left us with a ritual, and this ritual is to help us remember His teachings. What greater ritual could He leave us with? Live in God's word and live with the energy of love flowing through our bodies.

We are to become love and continually be love. The greatest of all commandments is to love!

The ritual Jesus left us with, gives us the best advice possible, and to this day this ritual is remembered and practiced.

Jesus continues to amaze me! He is brilliant, as He left us with this ritual for us to remember God's greatest commandments. If we simplify the Bible down to its most important teachings, there you have it in a nutshell, to live God's word and to be love, as God and Jesus are.

What Do We Look Like?

I awoke to Jesus speaking to me. He said, "Look." and I looked. I saw the Father, Son, and Holy Ghost, with Jesus sitting on the right hand of God, and the Holy Spirit sitting on the left hand of God. All three of them had long white hair and long white beards.

Then, Jesus instructed me to look again. This time, I saw three energy beings wearing long white robes, and they had golden light eyes.

Jesus instructed me to look again, and I saw the three of them dressed like my sons would dress. They were wearing flip-flops, shorts, and polo shirts. They were dressed like almost any 25- to 35-year-old and were also neat and well groomed.

Then, it was explained to me that many people picture God, the Son, and the Holy Spirit as three old men with white hair and long white beards. When they are working and sometimes appear to people, they appear wearing their working clothes, which are long white robes, and they're in energy form; hence, golden light eyes.

In the last scene they showed me how they might look when they are simply walking among us; they dress in a similar fashion, clean shaven.

By the way, they do walk among us.

Healing Eyes: The Look of Love

Last night Jesus answered a prayer of mine. I was asking for help on how to help my husband get rid of a
virus. He had come down with a bad cold. I wanted to
do energy work on him to get rid of the virus. I didn't
know how to get to it without waking him up, because
he was lying on his stomach and the virus was in his
chest not too far from his heart. If he had been lying
on his back it would have been easier for me to do the
energy work on him.

I was so excited when Jesus appeared to answer my
prayer for help. There are many wonderful healers that
might have answered my prayer from the Other Side.
Jesus immediately removed the virus in a way that I
hadn't learned just yet. I was in awe. Jesus explained
that the method he used is a stronger method than the
one I know.

He told me how to do this. First, you send the White
and Golden Light from your heart to just behind your
eyes. Next, you pull in additional sky sparkles through
your pineal gland at the top of your head. Then, you
send this energy to just behind your eyes. Then, mix
the two energies together and send them out through
your eyes to your target with its mission or intention,
such as remove the virus.

This mixture of Light from your heart and from the sky

sparkles creates a massive amount of White and Golden energy. Send this golden energy to penetrate the virus. Hence, the virus ceases to exist.

I've seen this before, a very long time ago. I thought they were Angels who were dressed in white robes, and that they had golden light eyes. Their eyes looked like light bulbs lit up. Now I understand what I saw: healers from heaven.

I tried to do this to repeat what I'd just learned from Jesus. I did a good job with the White and Golden Light from my heart, but I summoned up a limited amount of White Light from the sky sparkles through my pineal gland.

Until then, I will practice, practice, and then practice some more. I've been trying to learn how to get rid of viruses, and now I've been taught how to do it. There's always something new to learn and practice; I'll never get bored. There are some of you out there who might be naturals at this. See what you can do with this information.

Jesus died on the cross

God has proven His love for us. Now, He expects us to get it and be kind, generous, patient, and forgiving of others. Just follow the Golden Rule: Do unto others as you would have them do unto you! Be kind and caring of all.

Jesus explained that in Old Testament times, there were no laws for man to follow until God sent his Commandments through Moses. Then people were responsible to live by God's Laws. Later, Jesus died on the cross to forgive our sins. He descended into hell for three days and when He came out, He brought everyone with him. They were put back into the process of reincarnating.

Because of Jesus' forgiveness those who had gone to hell now have been reincarnating. Everyone who had gone to hell was given a second chance to reincarnate and spiritually advance. This is how inclusive Jesus' forgiveness is. Maybe they have spiritually improved; maybe not.

CHAPTER NINETEEN

My Favorite Sayings

I have some of my favorite sayings listed below. They make a point, hopefully in a palatable way. They seem to make sense to me and help me to make a responsible choice that will hopefully help me to spiritually advance, and successfully complete the lesson at hand. In my experience, the big life lessons seem to be a challenge. I'm reaching up to a new Level, and in order to get to the new Level, I must succeed. And I will succeed either sooner or later.

Sometimes there are lessons that I just really don't want to learn, and I'm not the only one. I've seen people put very important lessons on the back burner.

Usually, this lesson involves forgiveness. In fact, most divorces occur because one or the other of the couple involved refuses to forgive and sometimes the couple have finished their karma, and it's time for them to move on.

Remember, that as we forgive, we are forgiven. When forgiveness is chosen, the lesson has been completed, and the problem disappears, and the couple continues to be a couple. In this case, love was chosen over anger. Choosing to love is always the better answer.

I asked Jesus what the best way is to pray for others. He answered me that it is best to pray for Mercy. Mercy is unconditional love and is nonjudgmental and we leave the judging to Jesus and God.

The reason for having a past is to learn from it

So, once you learn something, move on. Isn't it fabulous that we can experience something, learn from it, and move on to something new? We don't have to continue forever and ever repeating the same lesson over and over once we master it correctly. Now, if we get the solution wrong, isn't it nice that we are given another chance to learn the correct answer, and not live throughout eternity making the wrong choice and stagnating?

Like attracts like

You attract friends who are like-minded. If you don't want to be like them or want to become something different don't hang around with them. Find new friends. This can prove to be either easy or difficult.

Life is easier if I hang around like-minded friends. If I meet a stranger who is like-minded, I seem to gravitate towards this person and usually become instant friends. Friends who I have something in common with may come and go, but a like-minded friend is a true friend for life in my experience.

Caring and kindness are the keys to "Love Thy Neighbor"

Follow the Golden Rule and you'll succeed in loving thy neighbor. This is the most important piece of information in this book. If you can get this, you can make it to higher Levels.

Everyone likes to be treated nicely. People don't like to be treated rudely or be insulted. If you care about someone, you will treat them nicely and show interest in them and be kind to them. If you meet a stranger, the right thing to do is to be kind to them. If you use the "Caring and Kindness" rule, you'll be nice to everyone. This is a good thing. Be gracious, "If it's not nice, don't say it" and if you don't want it to be repeated, don't say it. Just zip it. This will save you a lot of misery.

Listen to your heart

Your heart tells you the right thing to do because your heart knows the right answer. Your heart helps you to be kind and caring of others. Your heart chooses to for-give. If you're heart centered, then you're not angry. You can't be both heart-centered and angry at the same time. Listening to your heart will help you to have a happier and healthier life. There'll be less stress. This helps to avoid heart attacks or strokes. If you lis-ten to your heart, you'll make good choices that'll help you to spiritually advance. The whole purpose of life is to continually spiritually advance and raise your fre-quency higher and higher until you get to the next Level, and the next Level. Listen to your heart: it will help you do just that. When you are baptized the Holy Spirit enters your heart. Open both your heart and mind to God and you will belong to God. If you ask God to be part of your life with both your mind and heart open, the Holy Spirit will enter your heart and give you guidance and will live in your heart. Look to your heart for answers.

What you think is what you get

Only think what you wish to manifest. Thinking posi-tively helps you to co-create effectively. As I've ex-plained in an earlier chapter, you manifest whatever you think. So, this saying makes perfect sense. You think it, eventually you manifest it, and you're the one who lives with the result of your own thoughts. There it is: What you think is what you get!

Life is full of choices, so choose wisely

Each choice is a Moment of Truth. Have you chosen from the wisdom of your heart today? Each moment you are choosing and are either advancing or regressing. You have eternity to get wherever you're choosing to go. You're the one who lives with your choices and co-creates your life to be what it is.

If you don't like the life you've created, then change your choices and choose again. You can have a "do over" starting right from where you are at this moment. If you're in the habit of choosing wisely, keep it up, this is good for you and you'll be a good example to others!

Nancy J Balmert

CHAPTER TWENTY

The Next Phase: Like It or Not

In 1989 I was shown a vision of both past and future events. The pictures I was shown didn't have a date on them, so I don't know when any of what I saw will happen.

My vision started with a dinosaur ever so gently walking. His muscles were so powerful that he was light like a ballerina, and so brightly colored, a bright chartreuse color. Next, I was shown buildings coming down, as if an entire city had been bombed; this was New York City. I saw Yellowstone erupt. There was an unbelievable amount of ash and red-hot lava spewing out of the mountain.

I saw what looked like an atomic bomb. I didn't see the top of the explosion, but I believe that it was a nuclear bomb. I would try to stop it, but I'm not allowed to interfere. So, I don't even know where or when it will happen.

Then I was shown land that was flat and brown, with no vegetation. I saw a comet land in the water. I saw many earthquakes in this vision, and many volcanoes erupting. I saw a tsunami hit land.

After all this devastation, I was shown a banquet table full of fabulous food. I remember there being shrimp, pineapple, and loads of other fresh foods, bread, and wine.

So, the ocean life will survive, the grain belts will recover, and we will have plenty.

Some of these things I was shown, like 9/11, have happened. I was sitting in a chair at the dentist's office at the time of 9/11. I was probably the only one thanking God that the entire city wasn't destroyed.

Yellowstone doesn't need to blow, but if we stay on the course we're presently on, it is definitely going to blow. There are too many things have gone backwards in the United States. If Yellowstone blows, it will affect the 45th parallel, which is the grain belt. This could occur because of negative energy coming from all over the United States.

We must realize it is better to be self-reliant and not be a society wanting entitlements. We must get "off our duffs" and work hard to spiritually evolve. Those who have been successful can make donations to help those who are in need. This gives those who donate a chance to experience the Law of Multiplication.

A tsunami has occurred, and Haiti has had an earthquake.

There are more to come. I saw choirs of Angles singing in three different locations on the Earth. One of the locations was deep in the ocean and whales were singing right beside the Angels to break up the heavy vibrations that discombobulated humans are creating.

If we don't shape up and stop creating such heavy, black, toxic energy, the choirs of Angels will be commanded to stop singing. If that happens, in a very short period of time there will be a massive build-up of negative energy that will become a heavy weight on the Earth. The result will be chaos: volcanoes erupting and earthquakes.

Earth will start being cleaned up sooner than we think. All that negative energy will be transformed into positive energy, by breaking up the longer heavy wave lengths into shorter positive wavelengths. God and Jesus have command over what devastation happens to the Earth, not Satan, who is having his last hurrah.

The choices we are making right now will end up determining how much cleaning will need to be done. Man has created a great amount of negative energy: his karma is heavy on the Earth and will cause effects we won't like! If we shape up sooner, there will be less cleaning up to be done.

New Orleans did flood from hurricane Katrina. When I saw this earlier in a vision, I thought it was going to end up being little more than an oyster bay. Hurricane Katrina cleaned up a lot of negative energy in New Orleans. Katrina was sent to break up those long, heavy, negative frequencies into smaller, lighter frequencies. Many of the people who caused this negative energy relocated.

Houston had Hurricane Ike to clean up the heavy, negative energy that was deposited in a large area mainly by those who are negative who relocated from New Orleans. There were also many people relocated from New Orleans after Katrina, who are loving, wonderful, and light-hearted, salt of the earth type of people. These people are not responsible for the heavy frequencies that were brought to Houston. The hurricane transformed the heavy frequencies to light frequencies.

Negative people need to clean up their act. They've been dispersed and integrated into many different areas in small numbers. They may well choose to spiritually evolve or not. These people have massive negative thoughts, feelings, and emotions; Jesus has given them another chance to spiritually evolve.

God is a loving God, but it's time for everyone to follow God's Laws.

All of these spirits who are lower than Level One will be sent back to the Level they have achieved when they die, back to a lower species. No more reincarnating into human form unless they are at least a Level One.

This process could take a while. Most of Satan's followers will be uncomfortable with the Earth's higher frequency. Mother Earth is still raising her frequencies. Those who are vibrating on a lower frequency will choose to check out because they won't be able to handle the new higher frequencies. The last time Mother Earth raised her frequency, the Black Plague wiped out many lower developed spirits, or spirits with lower frequencies. Many higher frequency people chose to try to help others survive, and unfortunately also died from the plague.

Love or Hate

God and Jesus have been showing me the stress that negative energy has on the Earth.

Recently they took me far above the Earth, and what I saw was Mother Earth throbbing in pain. If only humans would be nice to their neighbor, instead of trying to control them, or cheat them, or steal from them, and worst of all hate them. Hate is a terrible thing. Now, you see rampant aggressive behavior. Lower vibrational people are violently protesting; and it's worse during a full moon. These people are filled with hate. Those who so intensely hate others will end up being turned to dust and lose their soul, deservedly so. God did not create people to misuse energy. In truth, there is only love. We need to fill ourselves with love.

All Four Elementals, Earth, Fire, Wind, and Water are helping Mother Earth by cleaning up negative energy. The Elementals help Mother Earth by breaking up lower frequencies, which become high frequencies. As Earth moves up to higher and higher frequencies, the Elementals are working hard to break up the lower frequencies. So, there are hurricanes, Earthquakes, Fires, and volcanoes that will erupt. Some are calling this climate change when it's Earth changes.

If you have noticed, there have been several hurricanes that hit towns with casinos. Smoking, gambling, and using drugs lowers people's vibrations or frequencies. Casinos tend to attract people who have these addictions.

Eventually there will be a change for the better because people will start changing. Those who want something for nothing will find out that there isn't a free ride. They will understand that everyone must pitch in and earn their own way.

If on the other hand, people start working harder on being self-reliant and responsible, and start cleaning up their own messes, there'll be no need for Mother Earth to go through such a drastic cleansing of negative, toxic, heavy energy.

This is our choice: to choose love, kindness, generosity, and patience, or to choose greed, lust, anger, slothfulness, gluttony, pride, envy, and a long list of other negatives. Love and kindness will help to usher us into a new era of peace.

• • • • • • • •

We are going through the process of the Judgement. It is going to take a while. Pray for peace. Pray to eliminate Socialism, Marxism, Communism, dictatorships, and all forms of governments that slow down spiritual growth. We've been the fastest spiritually developing planet in the universe. In the US our motto is "In God We Trust".

Finally, there is "The Rapture." Those who have opened their hearts and minds to God and have reached a level of perfection will ascend to Level Four in physical form. I've been told by God and Jesus, that people will start ascending during my lifetime. If you want to ascend in physical form like Enoch, Elijah, Mother Mary, or Buddha, then you need to love perfectly. I think that people will ascend when they have individually perfected unconditional love and forgiving instantly.

God spoke

On Sept 12, 2014, I woke up early and was told to go to my computer to take down a message from God. At 4:42 AM, after listening and typing it into my computer, I asked God if I could edit the message and move things around to put them into a different order. The answer was NO: readers will pay more attention to the message in the order He gave it to me. This is the message:

"Good morning, I am God your Father. I have come to tell you what you are supposed to be doing during your lifetime. You are supposed to be learning to love one another. In other words, learning to love thy neighbor as my son Jesus taught you. You are hesitant to learn this because you are failing in your endeavors. Be considerate of your neighbor. Be conscious of what you say to them and how you treat them.

I am disappointed that so many of you are so self-centered and not loving and giving to others. Giving is to be done through donations, not through taxes. If you vote higher taxes in for someone else to pay, you will be debited. You are slow to learn. Life is not a free ride.

You are here to spiritually advance; not to regress back down to fish or the amoeba. I want you to learn how to take care of yourself first; then how to help others. This is a demand, not a request. Again, I am God your creator and I know how you can advance the fastest. You have been on a slow ride. It is time for repentance, or you will receive your due: justice will be done. The time is here for judgment.

I am present at all times. I am larger than you can ever imagine.

You still have time to make things good; to repent, to help others, to learn to love Me, my Son, yourself, and others. Time is ticking. The scroll seals are being broken. You can avoid the consequences of your bad behaviors.

I am God your Father and the time for justice is here."

It is time to listen to God!

Let there be NO ifs, ands, or buts about it: God is God, and that is that. On Planet Earth, He is our God.

Nancy J Balmert

218

CHAPTER TWENTY-ONE

THE TIME OF CONSEQUENCES

In the Fall of 2019, I was told by the Other Side that we are now in the time of consequences, when what's been hidden will start to be revealed, things such as cheating, stealing, taking bribes, bribing others and in general, wrongdoing. Look around, and you will notice that the truth is being found out. Eventually there will be consequences from both man's laws and God's laws. Some of this is taking a while due to the procedure of the Judgement.

Whether or not people realize it, behaviors have con-sequences. When we do good things, those who watch over us take note. They keep a tally of both the good things we do and the undesirable things that we do. Let me reiterate, whatever you are thinking, saying, and doing is being recorded on your lifeline at every moment. You will be rewarded for your loving behaviors and penalized for negative behaviors. The good things we do are recognized, and something good comes back to us at the best time possible. If we do something bad or undesirable, there are negative consequences and something bad comes back to us just when we don't want it. Remember: we are now in the time of consequences when what's been hidden will be revealed!

Jesus came to teach us the key to a happy life: love thy neighbor. This covers pretty much everything. Treat each person with love, kindness, caring, patience, and generosity.

Jesus has already judged the dead and is now judging the living. The living have now been judged either Worthy or Not Worthy yet. Those who have been judged not worthy yet, have the rest of their lifetime to become Worthy. The easy way to become Worthy is to be baptized.

I love God. I love Jesus and everything He has done for us. I'm on a path to become perfect love; although I'm not there yet. If I were perfect, I wouldn't be here. I hope to ascend in physical form in this lifetime. I hope that many people will.

I'm hoping that all my relatives make it in this lifetime; that way we can go through eternity together. If some of them don't make it this time, they will reincarnate, develop a new brain, and have different memories in their brains with the reincarnated body. Their previous life history will be on their lifeline.

Here is a good rule to go by. to help If you with your choices. If don't want anyone to know what you're doing wrong, the answer is simple: don't do it! If you don't want something you said repeated, then don't say it!

For those who fail to learn to love thy neighbor, there are consequences. God says He has given enough time for people to choose. Enough is enough. God has been patient and so has Jesus, who gave up his life to teach us to love thy neighbor.

By the end of the Judgement evil will be wiped off the face of the Earth, and we will move into 1,000 years of peace. Just pause for a moment and think about how nice it's going to be with Evil gone. Planet Earth will be a place filled with peace and love! Hmmm...feels good! No more dishonest, hateful, cheating, or lying people.

Nancy J Balmert

CHAPTER TWENTY-TWO

The Idea

God came up with the idea that maybe people will advance faster with both intelligence and the ability to love. It turns out that we are advancing faster than any of the groups who are ahead of us. It has now been accepted that both love and intelligence is needed for groups to not get "stuck" on Level Five. What can I say, God is brilliant.

That brings me to another subject. Lucifer. He wanted to be chosen to be the "God" over earth, Lucifer and his followers thought that God's plan for advancing wouldn't work and set out prove God wrong by tempting people to do wrong and evil things. And so it goes... Lucifer has many followers who enjoy being pranksters and enjoy breaking the rules. Now, how many people have cheated on their spouses? How many people are dishonest? How many people cheat on their taxes? How many people have addictions? And then there are things like voting fraud, cover ups of miscellaneous kinds, and hiding the truth.

There is a hierarchy on the Other Side, and God is at the top of the highest Level, He is God of all.

As I noted earlier, there are a total of 32 groups, with our group being the newest group. Several groups are stuck on Level 5 and can't make it to Level 6.

Long ago God decided He would oversee the development of Planet Earth instead of delegating it to Zeus. Zeus would have been the one to choose who would get to do this and Lucifer was hoping to be chosen. God's plan would only advance those of us on planet Earth by both Love and Intelligence. Lucifer was angry and told God that His plan wouldn't work; that people would choose to be evil over learning to forgive unconditionally. So, God said if Lucifer turned out to be wrong, and God's plan turns out to be successful, that Lucifer would spend 1,000 years in hell.

Two thousand plus years ago, Jesus was born to Mary, who had been on the same Level as God. Mary was born to her mother on earth, Anne. Mary was an older soul and was given the responsibility to raise Jesus. Jesus brought with Him the knowledge that He had known from the higher Level. From the time Jesus was born, He was one with God. He knew God's thoughts and God knew Jesus' thoughts.

God is still overseeing planet Earth. It has been determined that God's plan is successful, and the groups stuck on Level Five are now able to proceed. Satan will spend 1,000 years in hell. There are many of Satan's (Lucifer's) followers who have choosen not to follow God. They don't follow His laws. They do evil things. Evil is as evil does! Not to worry; they will be judged for their doings at the time of their deaths.

Justice will be served!

CHAPTER TWENTY-THREE

The Judgement

This is the time of the Judgement. It started Dec 12, 2012, with the remaining ghosts being sent to the Level of the amount they had individually become. Now, things that people did are slowly being revealed. Starting in 2020 Jesus judged those who are alive as a human Level 1, 2, or 3 as either Worthy or Unworthy. If you have been baptized, no matter how good or bad you've been, you were judged as Worthy. If your hearts and minds were both open to God, then you were judged Worthy. If you have not been baptized in the name of the Father, Son, and Holy Spirit/Ghost, and your heart and mind are closed to God, then you were judged Un-worthy. Not to worry, you have eternity to open you heart and mind to God, or to be baptized. This Judge-ment process took a while.

Then, in the summer of 2022 the next phase of the judgement started. Beginning with the Worthy at the top of the most faithful and obeying, people were given merits and demerits. These have been collected by your Guides and stored up for you. These include all the good things you've done since Jesus died on the cross, and all the bad or undesirable things you have done.

What happens is you go before Jesus to be judged. You receive a judgement of a specific number of merits or demerits. If you have not been judged yet, you will be. You have until the end of your natural lifetime to earn more merits or demerits. At the time of your death, you will be given your final judgement. You will be sent to the amount of love or lack thereof that you have become. I'm told that people who attain perfect love will ascend to Level Four in physical form in this life-time at the time they accomplish this. It is necessary to have a physical form to be able to advance to Level Five.

Those who have been baptized but have immense amounts of demerits will keep their lifeline in the Akashic record room but will go back to the amoeba and have a "do over". Those who have been completely evil and have not been baptized will lose their lifeline in the Akashic record room and will lose their soul. Their evil energy will be detoxed/purified to be re-used, hopefully in a positive and loving way. All that will remain of them will be a smidge of dust.

Those who are advancing will have eternity to ascend in physical form.

To summarize:

Jesus wants us to be the embodiment of love; this is unconditional love. Becoming the embodiment of love is what being born again" means. It's being born of the spirit of love. When this happens, you move from the laws of gravitation to the laws of levitation, and you ascend in physical form to Level Four. This is what we are here on earth to accomplish, being a Master of Love.

Nancy J Balmert

ABOUT THE AUTHOR

The author *of Moments of Truth: A Tour of the Other Side* has a Masters-degree in Studies of the Future. She is also an accomplished artist, with her paintings depicting scenes from the many places she has traveled to all over the world. Her large flower paintings have won critical acclaim as International Artist of the Year. Her work can be seen on her website, **NancyBalmert.com.**

She married the love of her life in 1974; that's over 50 years ago. She is the mother of two married sons and has three grandchildren.

Nancy J Balmert

Moments of Truth: A Tour of the Other Side

Nancy J Balmert

Moments of Truth: A Tour of the Other Side

Nancy J Balmert